P.J. CLOVER · PRIVATE EYE
The Case of the Borrowed Baby

Also by Susan Meyers

P.J. CLOVER • PRIVATE EYE
The Case of the Missing Mouse

P.J. CLOVER • PRIVATE EYE
The Case of the Stolen Laundry

P.J. CLOVER · PRIVATE EYE
The Case of the Borrowed Baby
by Susan Meyers

illustrated by Gioia Fiammenghi

LODESTAR BOOKS
E. P. Dutton · New York

Library of Congress Cataloging in Publication Data

Meyers, Susan.
    P.J. Clover, private eye—the case of the borrowed baby/
by Susan Meyers: illustrated by Gioia Fiammenghi.
      p. cm.
    "Lodestar Books."
    Summary: P.J. and Stacy investigate a jewelry store heist
and a mystery involving a missing doll.
    ISBN 0-525-67247-8
    [1. Mystery and detective stories.] I. Fiammenghi, Gioia, ill.
II. Title. III. Title: Case of the borrowed baby.
PZ7.M5719Paaab 1988   87-27258
[Fic]—dc19   CIP
                                         AC

Published in the United States by E. P. Dutton,
2 Park Avenue, New York, N.Y. 10016,
a division of NAL Penguin Inc.

Published simultaneously in Canada by
Fitzhenry & Whiteside Limited, Toronto

Editor: Rosemary Brosnan

Printed in the U.S.A.   COBE   First Edition
10 9 8 7 6 5 4 3 2 1

for Jane Slack, a friend indeed

Contents

1   No More Dolls   1
2   The Perfect Crime   10
3   Want To Bet?   23
4   The Terrible Toomeys   33
5   Stolen!   43
6   Serious Stuff   54
7   Lapis Lazuli   63
8   A College Education   73
9   A Warning   81
10   The Perfect Disguise   97
11   Trapped!   108
12   The Final Operation   116

1
No More Dolls

Crime!

That was what P.J. Clover wanted.

We were in our headquarters, which used to be our clubhouse, on a Thursday afternoon. Our schoolbags were dumped in a corner. A pitcher of lemonade and a plate of pickle and peanut butter sandwiches (one of P.J.'s favorite combinations) were on the table.

But we weren't eating.

Not that *I* would have eaten pickles and peanut butter anyway!

We—or rather, *I* was listening. Listening to P.J. Clover rant and rave.

"It's no good, Stacy!" she exclaimed, grabbing a sandwich and biting into it. "No good at all!"

A shower of crumbs and a piece of pickle fell onto her Wonder Woman T-shirt and tumbled to the floor.

But P.J. didn't care.

P.J. Clover is *not* a girl who cares about pickles and crumbs on the floor.

P.J. Clover is a girl with bigger things—*much* bigger things—on her mind. Things like . . .

"Crime!" Her eyes lit up as she said the word, and she started to pace back and forth. "Crime, Stacy, that's what we need. *Real* crime!" She flicked a strand of straggly blond hair out of her eyes. "He wouldn't call us doll-hounds if we solved a *real* crime. He wouldn't dare!"

So that was it! I might have known. When P.J. gets upset, there's usually one person—and one person only—behind it: Butch Bigelow!

Butch, in case you haven't heard, is P.J. Clover's nemesis. That means he's her enemy or, at any rate, her rival. And this doll-hound business was just his latest way of getting under her skin.

"But don't you see—" I began.

I was going to say that Butch was jealous. Jealous of us for setting up a successful private eye business.

I was going to say that his nose was out of joint because we'd solved a case in which *he* was the victim. (You can read about that in *The Case of the Missing Mouse.*)

Butch had promised then that he'd stop bothering us, but promises like that are hard to keep. Especially when we'd continued to solve cases. Especially when P.J., who's not exactly modest, had continued to brag about the cases we solved.

That was what I was going to say. But P.J. didn't give me a chance. Not that it would have mattered. Because it was the cases we'd been solving that were the problem.

"That's the worst of it," she said, flopping into the

grungy old beanbag chair that took up one whole corner of the clubhouse—sorry, but headquarters is too hard to remember—and gulping down the rest of her sandwich.

Her long skinny arms and legs stuck out at angles like a grasshopper's.*

"I hate to say it," P.J. said, "but this time Butch Bigelow is right. Dolls—dumb old, boring old dolls!—are *exactly* what we've been tracking down!"

She jumped up and grabbed the wire basket sitting on the table, beside the lemonade.

"Listen to this," she said, pulling the top file from the basket and starting to read, "Client: Debbie Potts. Case: Lost Raggedy Ann. Solution: Found under the rosebushes where the dog hid it. Or this one . . ." She tossed the first file aside and grabbed another folder from the basket. "Client: Lisa Lipschutz. Case: Lost Barbie. Solution: Found in a box of old clothes ready to go to Goodwill. Or this—"

"Now, wait a second," I interrupted. You have to

---

*Don't worry. I'm not going to have a lot of footnotes. But I want to explain—before I get too far into things—that besides being P.J. Clover's best friend and partner, I, Stacy Jones, am a writer.

And my creative writing teacher (Mrs. Crane, fifth grade, Park School, Mill Creek, California) says we should do stuff like that. Compare people's arms and legs to grasshopper's arms and legs, I mean. She says it makes for vivid writing.

But I won't do too much of it. Not enough to slow down the action!

Now, go back to where you were. With P.J. Clover in the beanbag chair.

interrupt with P.J. Otherwise she'll go on forever. And besides, I was getting annoyed. Annoyed with the way she was tossing files around. Annoyed with the way she was *agreeing* with Butch Bigelow!

"What's wrong with finding dolls?" I said. "Debbie Potts and Lisa Lipschutz were happy, weren't they? They got their dolls back, didn't they? That's what's important, isn't it?"

P.J. didn't reply.

In fact, I don't think she heard a word I said. Because as I was talking, her eyes had suddenly lit upon the newspaper lying on the table. It was today's *Morning Gazette*. I'd brought it out from P.J.'s house—our clubhouse is in the Clovers' backyard—along with the lemonade because P.J. always manages to spill and I've found that newspaper is good for mopping up. (A Stacy Jones household hint!)

Anyway, as I was going on about finding dolls and making little girls happy, P.J. was staring at the front page of the paper. And as she stared, several peculiar things—peculiar in anyone but P.J., that is—began to happen. First, her eyes began to sparkle. Then her cheeks began to glow. And then her nose gave a twitch exactly like a rabbit's.

She grabbed the paper from the table, almost knocking over the lemonade. "Stacy!" she exclaimed. "This is it! *Exactly* what we've been looking for!"

"What do you mean?" I said. I hadn't known we were looking for anything, and I hadn't even glanced at the paper when I brought it out.

"This story," P.J. replied excitedly. "On the front page. It says that—"

4

But before she could finish her sentence, there was a sudden pounding on our clubhouse door.

"Open up!" a voice shouted.

P.J. shot a quick glance at me, then put her eye to the peephole in the door. It's drilled through the wood and comes out right smack in the center of the picture of an eye that's hung on the other side.

"I see you," I heard the voice say as P.J., suddenly looking as if she'd like to disappear—or at least bolt out the window—stepped away from the door. "Open up! I've got a case for you to solve."

"P.J., who is it?" I whispered.

But before she had a chance to reply, the door was shoved open, pinning P.J. to the wall, and I saw for myself.

It was Tina Toomey, the brattiest—to put it mildly—four year old in the neighborhood.

"Where's the eye?" she demanded, stepping into the clubhouse and planting her plump little hands on her plump little hips. She was wearing blue denim overalls embroidered with red strawberries, and she looked for all the world like an overstuffed blueberry with a bad case of measles. "The *real* eye," she added, fixing me with an accusing stare.

I was about to say that *I* was a real eye, even though my name comes beneath P.J.'s on the clubhouse door, but then I thought better of it. Tina is famous for her tantrums, and I didn't want to trigger one now.

Luckily, P.J., who's not one to shirk responsibility, squeezed herself out from behind the door where Tina had trapped her.

5

"You have a case?" she said, eyeing Tina suspiciously. "What kind of a case?"

And all at once, Tina collapsed.

I don't mean she fell on the floor or anything like that. But she looked as if the wind had gone out of her sails. She sagged, sort of like a balloon that's lost its air. Her lower lip, which had been sticking out in a pout, trembled. Her voice cracked.

"It's . . . it's my baby," she stammered, tears suddenly welling up in her eyes. "My . . . my Baby Cuddles!"

P.J.'s eyebrows shot up. "I knew it!" she said, turning to me. "It's a doll! Another doll!"

Tina winced at the words. And I couldn't help feeling sorry for her, even if she was a pest. Because I knew that, to her, Baby Cuddles wasn't just a doll. She was a baby. A *real* baby.

Which isn't so surprising since Baby Cuddles happens to be one of those lifelike dolls that drinks and eats and wets and . . . Well, let's just say you get to change her diapers exactly like a real parent does!

Anyway, messy or not, Tina loved her. And I could see that she was going to be miserable—and probably make everyone else miserable too—until she got her back.

"Can you tell us where you last saw her?" I asked quickly, pulling a wrinkled-up tissue from my pocket and handing it to her.

But P.J. had had enough.

"No!" she exclaimed. "Stacy, we are *not* in the doll-finding business anymore! We're going to solve a crime." She waved the newspaper she'd been about to show me before Tina arrived in my face. "A *real* crime!" And with that, she grabbed me by the arm and dragged me out of the clubhouse, down the steps, and across the backyard to the driveway where our bikes were parked.

"But . . . but my baby," Tina cried.

"Sorry," P.J. called, swinging one of her long skinny legs over the seat of her bike and pushing off.

"But I need her!" Tina shouted. An ominous note had crept into her voice. "Now!" She stamped down the clubhouse steps and started across the yard in our direction.

I could see that, in a moment, the storm would break. In a moment, she'd be on the ground, kicking and screaming and holding her breath until she turned blue in the face. And all at once, following P.J.—*wherever* she was going—seemed like exactly what I wanted to do.

I hopped onto my bike. "Look in the clothes hamper," I called, trying to sound sympathetic as I pushed off. We'd found lots of missing dolls in clothes hampers. "Check under the rosebushes."

Swinging into the street after P.J., I heard Tina begin to howl—a long, earsplitting wail that would have put any self-respecting timber wolf to shame. I was glad to have a pair of rapidly moving wheels under me.

P.J. was already halfway down the block. Her straggly blond hair was blowing in the breeze; the newspaper was flapping in her bike basket.

Pedaling like crazy, I caught up.

"P.J., what's in that paper?" I panted as Tina's howls grew dim in my ears. "Where are we going? What's going on?"

8

P.J. didn't slow down. P.J. Clover never slows down. Not when she's got something big on her mind! But she did reach into her bike basket and pass the newspaper to me.

"It's all there," she yelled over her shoulder as she pulled ahead again. "Findletter's Jewelry Store. Right here in Mill Creek. It's been robbed!"

2

The Perfect Crime

It's not easy to read a newspaper while you're riding a bicycle.

In fact, it's impossible.

And so all I could do before we reached the jewelry store was make out the headline, FINDLETTER'S ROBBED!, and the comment that followed, Police Baffled.

But that was enough.

Enough to make me think that *this* time P.J. Clover might be biting off more than she could chew.

"What makes you think we can solve this?" I said breathlessly, when after ten minutes of furious pedaling we reached the center of town and swung our bikes into the passageway between Findletter's and the pet shop next door. "It's a real crime. Even the police are baffled."

"Exactly!" said P.J., who couldn't have had a chance to read much more of the newspaper story than I had. "That's what makes it so perfect! No more Raggedy

Anns, no Barbies, no Baby Cuddles for us," she said, hopping off her bike and tucking the ends of her Wonder Woman T-shirt into her jeans. "Butch Bigelow's not going to be able to call us any more names. Not this time, he's not!"

She set the kickstand on her bike and headed for the front door of the jewelry shop. She had a look in her eyes that said there was no stopping her, but I tried anyway.

After all, *someone* has to keep her feet on the ground in this business!

"P.J., wait," I called.

I was going to point out that a case like this could be dangerous. (Anyone who would rob a jewelry store sounded dangerous to me!)

I was going to mention that Mill Creek had a police force to take care of things like this, though they did happen to be baffled at the moment. I was even going to suggest that we go back to Tina Toomey.

But it was no use. P.J. had already pushed open the door and disappeared inside. All I could do—all I could *ever* do with P.J., it seemed!—was follow.

The inside of Findletter's seemed dark—dark and spooky, *I* thought—after the bright sunlight outside, and I heard a familiar voice say "Stacy Jones!" before I could make out anything more than the shadowy silhouette of a slender young woman standing behind the counter. Then, as my eyes adjusted to the light, I saw who it was—Annalise Brown, my favorite counselor from summer camp.

"Annalise!" I exclaimed. "What are you doing here? I thought you were in college."

At that, the smile that had come to her face when

11

she saw me disappeared. "I was," she said quickly, "but I had to drop out because I couldn't afford it anymore. I'm trying to earn enough money to go back, but now . . ." She paused, and suddenly I noticed that her eyes were red, as if she'd been crying. "But now, I don't know," she rushed on, sounding not at all like the confident Annalise I remembered from the volleyball courts at camp. "If that necklace that was stolen yesterday isn't found, I may be out of a job!"

P.J. shot me a glance. And it wasn't hard for someone who knows her as well as *I* do to guess what she was thinking.

Not only had there been a robbery . . .

Not only was there a crime to solve . . .

But there was a person in distress.

It was *exactly* the sort of situation that P.J., who identifies with the figure on her T-shirt—Wonder Woman, remember—likes best!

She stepped forward eagerly, pulling a small white card from the back pocket of her blue jeans. "I believe we can help," she said, handing the card to Annalise.

It was one of our business cards, of course. A newspaper reporter had them printed up for us when we solved our first case. They look like this:

P.J. CLOVER • PRIVATE

NO CASE TOO LARGE
NO CASE TOO SMALL

Stacy Jones, associate
phone 388–9456

Pretty impressive, I think. But Annalise didn't look impressed, she looked confused. She glanced from the card to P.J., taking in the straggly blond hair, the Wonder Woman T-shirt, the elbows and knees that seemed to stick out all over the place. "Well, I don't know," she murmured hesitantly. "This is a real crime, you know, not a lost doll or"—I saw P.J. grit her teeth!—"or a missing Teddy bear or something. Why, even the police don't have a clue . . . except what *I* could tell them."

"You mean . . ." P.J. seemed to forget about lost dolls and missing Teddy bears. "You were here when it happened? You're an *eye witness*?"

"I'm the *only* witness," Annalise replied rucfully (which means she wished it weren't so). "That's why Mr. Findletter holds *me* responsible!"

"You?" I said. "But that's not fair!" I didn't know much about the case yet, but I knew injustice when I saw it. "Anyone could be robbed. It couldn't have been *your* fault."

"But that's just it!" Annalise exclaimed, her eyes filling with tears. "It was! Not that I meant for it to be. After all, how was I to know . . . I mean, she seemed so . . . I never would have thought that . . . But I guess I'm not making much sense!"

P.J. stepped in quickly.

"Don't worry about that," she said, as if Annalise were a fish that she had on her line and didn't want to let slip away. "Just tell us what happened as it happened, and *we'll* make sense of it.

"Have you got your notebook?" she whispered to me.

Of course I did. A writer is *never* without her notebook!

13

I pulled it from my pocket, and feeling ashamed of myself for not wanting to get involved in the first place (when someone like Annalise Brown was in trouble!), I got ready to make up for it by taking down everything she had to say.

For a moment, Annalise hesitated. "Well, I don't know," she murmured, a worried look in her eyes. "I'm not sure he'd . . ." But then, seeing me with my notebook and pencil ready and P.J. with a determined look on her face, she gave in. "Oh, all right," she agreed, managing a faint smile. "I guess it can't hurt, and maybe it will help. Kids sometimes see things that grown-ups miss. That's what the boy I was baby-sitting for last night said. He made me tell him every last detail and . . . But you don't want to hear about that."

She must have noticed the impatient expression on P.J. Clover's face!

"You want to hear about the robbery. Well, I'm afraid it wasn't very dramatic. Nothing like what you see on TV. In fact, I didn't even know it was a robbery until it was over and by then it was too late. You see, what happened . . ."

Unfortunately, there's not room to print all of my notes here. They go on for pages! So what I'll do is give you a synopsis (that's a kind of shortened version) of what Annalise had to say. Basically, what it came down to was this:

The robbery—which Annalise didn't know was a robbery—began on Wednesday, October 19th at around three o'clock, when the thief—who Annalise didn't know was a thief—came into the store. She was a young woman with bright red hair, wearing sunglasses

14

with rhinestone-studded frames, long white gloves, and some kind of dark-colored dress.

"I'm afraid I didn't pay much attention to the dress," Annalise explained. "Not with all that other stuff to look at!"

"Obviously a disguise," P.J. said quickly. "But was there anything that you recognized? Underneath the sunglasses and all. Could she have been someone you knew, someone who'd been in the store before?"

"I don't *think* so," Annalise replied hesitantly. "She had an accent—French, I think—and I don't remember anyone French coming into the store. And yet, there *was* something. I can't quite put my finger on it, but . . . Of course, I may be imagining things," she added quickly. "At least, that's what the police seemed to think."

"Hmph," P.J. snorted.

And I knew she was thinking—as private eyes *always* seem to think—that the police might be wrong. That they just might be missing something important.

"Underline that," she whispered as Annalise continued.

But of course I already had. P.J. Clover's not the only one who's on the ball in this business!

The next thing that happened, Annalise said, was that the woman asked if Mr. Findletter was in, and when Annalise told her he wasn't, she seemed disappointed.

Which seemed strange to me. I mean, if *I* were going to rob a jewelry store, I'd be *happy* if the owner wasn't in!

I could see that P.J. was thinking the same thing.

15

She looked over my shoulder to see if I was underlining again—which I was—and then turned back to Annalise.

"What did she do next?" she asked. "After you told her Mr. Findletter wasn't in."

"Well, for a moment, she didn't seem to know what to do," Annalise replied. "But then, she started looking around the shop. She was very dramatic, exclaiming over this and that. Almost as if she were acting a part in a play. Finally, she noticed a necklace Mr. Findletter had just bought from a man who's been coming in lately to sell him things. I didn't think it was her style. Just dark blue beads with smaller gold ones in between and a funny little catch in the shape of a dolphin. But she seemed to like it."

By this time Annalise had begun to think that maybe the woman was some kind of eccentric millionaire. She figured she might make a big sale, not just of the blue necklace but of some other pieces in the store as well. She knew that would make Mr. Findletter— who'd been worried about money lately—happy, so, she was glad when the woman wanted to try the necklace on. She helped her fasten the catch and gave her a mirror to see how it looked.

Then something happened!

The woman began to cough. She clutched at her throat. She struggled for breath. "Water! Get me water!" she gasped.

Annalise was alarmed. She didn't want the woman to die right there in the middle of Findletter's Jewelry Store. So she ran to the back room and filled a glass with water from the sink in the lavatory. Then she ran back into the main part of the shop and . . .

16

"The woman was gone!" P.J. exclaimed. "Am I right?"

"I only wish that you weren't," Annalise replied. "Of course, at first, I didn't realize what had happened. I thought she'd collapsed, so I ran around the counter to see if she was lying on the floor. Then, when I saw that she wasn't there, it dawned on me. Findletter's had been robbed!

"I pushed the alarm button under the counter, and as the alarm started ringing, I ran outside. People came out of the other shops to see what was going on, and in a few minutes, the police arrived."

"But where did she go?" I said. "Didn't anyone see her? Someone with red hair, dressed the way she was, would be easy to spot."

"That's what you'd think," Annalise agreed. "But apparently no one did. At least, no one came forward to say that they did. The police searched the whole downtown area and didn't find a trace of her. It was as if she'd never existed. As if she just vanished into thin air!"

"*With* the necklace!" said P.J. She frowned. And I wondered if she was thinking, as I was thinking, that this case wasn't going to be so simple after all. That *we* might wind up just as baffled as the police!

If any such thoughts were going through P.J. Clover's head, she wasn't about to admit them, not even to me. Instead, she ran her hand over the countertop. "No fingerprints, of course," she murmured. "Not with those gloves she was wearing." She dropped to her hands and knees and began to crawl around on the rug.

"Clues," I explained quickly to Annalise, who looked

18

startled. "You'd be surprised what you can find on a floor."

But this time P.J.—even though she'd pulled her brand-new magnifying glass from her back pocket and held it over every inch of the carpet—came up empty-handed.

"I didn't think you'd find anything," Annalise said. "The police couldn't—"

But P.J. didn't want to hear what the police could or couldn't do. "Tell us about the necklace," she interrupted, as if she didn't care about not finding any clues. "You described how it looked, but what was it worth?"

I expected Annalise to quote a figure in the hundreds, maybe even thousands, of dollars. But to my surprise she said, "The peculiar thing is, I don't even know! You see, Mr. Findletter had just bought it. Then he was called out suddenly—by the attendance office at his daughter's school—and he left in a rush. The necklace wasn't priced and it wasn't on display. It was just sitting in an open box on the shelf behind the counter. If anyone had wanted to buy it, I wouldn't have known what to charge. I'd have had to wait until Mr. Findletter got back. You see, it was old and sort of ugly and—"

"Sounds like an antique," I said.

P.J. shot me an excited glance, and I could just imagine what she was thinking. Brilliant Girl Detective Finds Valuable Antique Necklace, her picture on the front page of the *Morning Gazette,* the police filled with gratitude, Butch Bigelow green with envy.

"Well, was it?" she asked eagerly. "A valuable antique? Is that why it was stolen?"

19

But again, Annalise wasn't sure. "That's what I thought at first," she replied, "because Mr. Findletter was so upset when he found out it was gone. But then, when the police were investigating, he played the whole thing down. It was almost as if he didn't want them to know about the necklace. As if he didn't want them to try to get it back. It's strange, isn't it? I just can't figure it out."

Neither could I. And even P.J., who usually comes up with lots of theories, seemed stumped. "Maybe he didn't want the publicity," she said, though she didn't sound very convinced. "Or maybe he didn't want to spend time talking to the police." She sounded even less convinced of that. "Or maybe . . ."

Suddenly, she stopped. Her eyes narrowed. "Maybe . . ." she said slowly.

But before she could pin down whatever it was, the door of the jewelry store opened and a short, bald, nervous-looking man walked in.

It was Mr. Findletter. I recognized him right away, not just from the jewelry store, but from various events around town—he's the head of the Chamber of Commerce, he sponsors a Little League team, that sort of thing. But I don't remember ever seeing him looking so tired and worried. It was as if he had the weight of the world on his shoulders.

"Annalise, has my daughter. . . ?" he began. Then he noticed P.J. and me. "Oh, sorry," he said. "I didn't realize you had . . . uh . . . customers."

"Oh, but we're not—" I started.

But P.J. beat me to it. "We're not shopping," she announced, stepping forward boldly. She pulled one of our cards out of her pocket and handed it to the store owner. "We're investigating!"

"The robbery," I explained quickly. "We think we may be able to—"

"You what?" The puzzled look that had come over Mr. Findletter's face when P.J. handed him the card was replaced by a look of alarm. "But you can't do that!" he exclaimed. He turned to Annalise. "What have you been telling them?" he said accusingly. "You should know better than to fill their heads with nonsense. This isn't a game. It's nothing for children to be involved in."

"Nothing for children—" P.J.'s eyes flashed. "Listen, we may be young, but . . ."

"They were only trying to help," Annalise protested.

And at that, something inside Mr. Findletter seemed to snap. "Well they can help someone else," he said angrily.

"But—" Annalise began.

"No buts about it. This is serious business. It could be dangerous." He shook his finger at P.J. and me. "I want you girls to stay out of it. Understand? Play your games somewhere else. And as for you," he addressed Annalise again, "I'll see you in my office in five minutes!" And with that, he turned on his heel and disappeared into the back room of the shop.

For a moment, P.J. was too stunned to move.

"Not a game," she sputtered. "Play somewhere else." Her fists clenched. She took a step toward the room where Mr. Findletter had disappeared, but I managed to hold her back.

"P.J., don't," I whispered, grabbing her by the back

21

of her Wonder Woman T-shirt. "You'll just get Annalise into trouble."

That stopped her, but it didn't calm her down.

"The nerve!" she fumed. "Well, we'll show him!"
There was a look of steely determination in her eyes.
"We'll find his old necklace and then—"

"Oh, but maybe he's right," Annalise murmured,
looking more upset than ever. (And echoing the
thought that had been going through my brain ever
since Mr. Findletter had mentioned danger.) "Maybe
it's not anything for you to be involved in. Maybe I
shouldn't have . . . And there's still Butch!" she said.

"Butch?" P.J. looked shocked. "You don't mean
. . . You couldn't mean . . .

"The boy I was baby-sitting for last night," Annalise
explained. "The one who wanted to know all about the
case. He said he'd come in this afternoon and— Oh,
dear," she broke off. "Wouldn't you know it? Here he
is now!"

3

Want To Bet?

Any hope I might have had that Annalise was talking about some other Butch disappeared as the door was flung open and a short—short in comparison with P.J., that is—freckle-faced, curly haired boy burst into the jewelry shop. His cheeks were red. His hair was tangled and sweaty. He looked as if he'd been running for blocks.

"Annalise!" he said breathlessly. "I've got something to—"

Then he saw P.J. and me.

"You!" he exclaimed, stopping dead in his tracks.

"You!" P.J. echoed.

"Then you know each other?" Annalise said.

"Yes," I replied quickly, since both P.J. and Butch Bigelow seemed to have been struck temporarily speechless. "We're . . ."

What could I say? Not enemies. I didn't feel like Butch Bigelow's enemy. And if what Annalise had said was true, and Butch wanted to help the same per-

son we wanted to help (namely, Annalise herself), I
didn't think that P.J. should be his enemy either.

"We're . . . uh . . . in the same class at school," I finally answered.

"Oh, good," Annalise murmured, casting a worried
glance in the direction of the room where Mr. Findletter had disappeared. "Then maybe you girls can take
Butch outside and explain."

But Butch wasn't about to be taken anywhere.

"No!" he said. "Wait!"

There was an urgent note in his voice. And all at
once, I noticed that he didn't look smart-alecky and
ready for a fight, as he usually did when he ran into
P.J. Clover. Instead, he looked worried. Worried,
and maybe even a little bit scared.

"I've got something to tell you," he said, ignoring
P.J. and me and turning to Annalise. "Something
important!"

"Important!" P.J. hooted, recovering her voice.
"What could *you* have to say that . . ."

"Shh, not so loud," Annalise warned. "Mr. Findletter will—"

But even as she spoke, the store owner called out
from the back room. "Annalise!"

"You'd better leave," Annalise whispered anxiously.
"Please."

"But . . ." Butch began.

"Annalise," Mr. Findletter called again. "I want to
see you. Now!"

And at that, *I* decided to take charge.

"Come on," I hissed, grabbing P.J. by the arm and
Butch by the back of his shirt. "Can't you see we're
going to get her in trouble?"

24

"But she's *already* in trouble!" Butch protested.

"What are you talking about?" P.J. demanded, as I dragged the two of them out the door and deposited them on the sidewalk outside. "Is this some kind of a stunt? Are you trying to make us look—"

"No!" Butch exclaimed. "For crying out loud. If you'd just stop thinking about yourself for a second and listen."

Something in his voice made P.J. pause. "To what?" she asked warily.

"To what I'm trying to tell you!" Butch exclaimed. He ran his fingers through his hair, making it stand up in curly brown tufts.

And suddenly, I felt sorry for him. He *was* trying to tell us something, and we weren't listening.

"What is it, Butch?" I said. "We know about the robbery. So if it has anything to do with that . . ."

"It has *everything* to do with that!" he exclaimed. "*And* with Annalise. She's in trouble, I tell you. Big trouble. She could be arrested. She could even go to jail!"

"Jail?" P.J. stared at Butch in disbelief. "What do you mean?" she said. "Why would Annalise Brown go to—"

"Because," Butch broke in, "the police think that *she* took that necklace!"

For a moment, neither P.J. nor I said a word. What could we say? Annalise Brown, my favorite counselor, a thief? It wasn't possible! "But . . . but that's crazy!" I finally managed to say. "Annalise would never . . ."

"How did you find this out?" P.J. demanded.

"I overheard it," Butch replied, looking relieved that someone—even if it was P.J. Clover—was finally tak-

25

ing him seriously. "I was in Dilly's Ice Cream Parlor and two police officers were in there. They were sitting in a back booth drinking coffee and talking about the robbery. One of them said it was strange that nobody but Annalise had seen the thief. And then the other one said, 'Yeah, it makes you wonder if there really was one.' He said he'd heard of cases where an employee stole from a store and invented a thief as a cover-up. At first they sort of joked about it. But then they got serious. They said they'd hate to believe it of her, but since there weren't any other leads, it just might be true. They said that maybe if nothing turned up by Saturday they'd have to—"

"By Saturday? But that's just two days away!" I said.

"Right," Butch agreed grimly. "That's why I've got to warn her. Maybe she can leave town. Maybe she can . . ." He started for the door of the jewelry store, but P.J. stopped him.

"Wait a second," she said, grabbing him by the arm before he could shove open the door. "Are you sure you heard right? Did they actually say they were going to arrest her? Did they really say they were going to put her in jail?"

Butch squirmed in her grip. An embarrassed look crept over his face. "Well . . . uh . . . no, not exactly," he admitted.

"Then don't be a dope!" P.J. exclaimed, letting go of his arm. "Right now they only suspect her. They figure they'll bring her in for questioning or something on Saturday. But if she left town . . . Well, how do you think that would look?"

Butch didn't reply, but I could see by the look on his face that he realized she was right.

26

"But P.J., we've got to do something," I said. "We can't just let them—"

"But we will!" P.J. interrupted, not seeming to realize that she was suddenly including Butch in our plans! "Listen," she said, "the only way we can really help her is by finding that necklace. So that's exactly what we're going to do! We'll . . ." But then she stopped. "That is, we will unless . . ." Her voice trailed off and an embarrassed look came over her face.

"Unless what?" Butch said.

"Well . . . uh . . ." P.J. stalled. She looked as if she were thinking something she didn't want to say.

And all at once I realized she must be thinking of the first rule of a private eye: *Trust no one . . . suspect everyone!* It was her favorite saying. She'd made it up herself, in fact. But this time she was taking it too far.

"Oh, no, P.J.," I said. "You *can't* suspect Annalise!"

"Suspect Annalise?" Butch looked at P.J. as if she'd gone out of her mind. "Are you nuts?" he said. "Why, she's been my baby— I mean . . ." He stopped himself just in time. (After all, no one in the fifth grade likes to admit to having a babysitter!) "I mean, I've known her for years," he said quickly. "She would never—"

"I didn't say she did," P.J. defended herself. "It's just that she *is* the only witness, and she *does* need money for college, and we *do* have to keep an open—"

"Well if that's what you think," Butch interrupted disgustedly, "you can just forget about working with me."

"Working with *you*?" P.J. stared at Butch in astonishment.

"That's right," he said. "Because I'm going to solve

27

this case. I thought you might want to help, but—"

"You've got to be kidding!" P.J. hooted. (The spirit of cooperation that I'd seen blossoming just a moment before flew out the window.) "You helping us is one thing. But *us* helping *you*? That's the craziest idea I ever heard!"

"Oh, it is, is it?" said Butch. He put his hands on his hips and stuck his chin out like a bulldog.

"That's right, it is," replied P.J., putting *her* hands on *her* hips and sticking *her* chin out.

I was reminded of all the contests—paste eating, breath holding, watermelon-seed spitting—that I'd witnessed between the two of them over the years.

"Now, wait a second," I said. "This isn't worth fighting about. Annalise needs help."

But Butch had gone too far. P.J. was beyond thinking about cooperation. "Oh, no," she said. "This is going to take brains. Brains and experience. And that leaves *you*, Butch Bigelow, out!"

"Oh, it does, does it?" said Butch, drawing himself up to his full height, which was still a head shorter than P.J. "Well, I wouldn't say that finding a bunch of dolls is the kind of experience that—"

But before he could go any further, a station wagon pulled up to the curb. Butch's mother was in the driver's seat.

"Butch Bigelow," she called, leaning over and opening the door on the passenger side. "I've been looking all over town for you. You've got a violin lesson in fifteen minutes!"

Butch turned red.

I guess violin lessons don't fit his image any better than babysitters do!

28

"Aw, Mom . . ." he groaned.

But Mrs. Bigelow paid no attention.

"Luckily, this street's not closed to traffic like it was yesterday," she said, sweeping a pile of library books off the seat to make room for Butch. "All these road repairs they've been making are so inconvenient and . . . For goodness' sakes, hurry up," she urged. "We haven't got all day."

"And neither do we!" said P.J. She gave Butch a shove—a none-too-gentle shove—in the direction of the car. "You just hurry along now," she said. "Don't keep your mother waiting." There was a wicked gleam in her eyes. A gleam that had appeared the moment Butch mentioned dolls. "Enjoy your violin lesson and don't worry about a thing. We'll have this case solved in no time!"

"In no time?" Butch stopped, half in and half out of the car. "Who do you think you're—"

"Well, maybe not in *no* time," P.J. admitted, the gleam still in her eyes. "But by Saturday. We'll have that necklace found by Saturday, or my name's not P.J. Clover, private eye!"

Butch looked as if he were about to choke. "By Saturday— Your name's not—" he sputtered. "Who do you think you're kidding, Clover? You'll never—"

"Want to bet?"

The words were out of P.J.'s mouth before I could stop her.

I opened my own mouth to object—P.J.'s betting had gotten us into plenty of trouble in the past—but it was too late. Butch was already accepting the challenge.

"Why not?" he replied, paying no attention to the hurry-up noises his mother was making from inside

29

the car. "What'll it be this time? Your allowance for a month? Your bug collection? Your—"

He stopped. He was staring at Wonder Woman leaping off P.J.'s T-shirt. "Wait a second! I've got it," he said. "Your T-shirts!"

P.J. gulped. "My . . . my T-shirts?" she repeated, turning a shade paler.

I think I must have turned pale, too. Because asking P.J. to put up her T-shirt collection was like asking the Queen of England to wager the crown jewels! P.J. has shirts from everywhere, shirts with all kinds of pictures and sayings on them. I couldn't imagine her without them. Why, in a plain white shirt, P.J. Clover wouldn't be P.J. Clover!

"Well, how about it?" Butch demanded. The gleam was in *his* eyes now. "You're the one who wanted to bet. You're the one who bragged you could do it. Of course, if you don't think you can . . ."

That was all P.J. needed.

"You're on," she said, throwing caution—and her T-shirts—to the wind.

Mrs. Bigelow revved up the engine.

Butch slid into the front seat and slammed the door.

"Wait!" I exclaimed. "Butch, you've got to . . ."

But it was too late. Mrs. Bigelow had already pulled away from the curb.

Butch pressed his nose against the window, put his thumbs in his ears, and waggled his fingers at us as the car sped away down the block. He looked ridiculous—ridiculous, but triumphant. Like someone who's just pulled a fast one and gotten away with it. Which, of course, is exactly what he'd done!

I whirled around to face P.J.

"Pamela Jean Clover," I said, not bothering to worry about what her reaction to her real name (which she hates!) might be, "do you realize what you've just done? You've just made a one-sided bet. You put up your T-shirt collection without getting Butch to put up a thing! He can't lose, P.J.," I said, groaning. "This time Butch Bigelow *can't lose!*"

4

The Terrible Toomeys

The look on P.J.'s face told me she realized I was right. But being P.J. Clover, she wasn't about to admit she'd made a mistake!

"Wrong, Stacy," she said, pulling herself together. "*We're* the ones who can't lose!"

She tucked the ends of her Wonder Woman T-shirt into her jeans (it had been in her collection so long it was just about outgrown) and headed for her beat-up old three-speed still parked between Findletter's and the pet shop next door. "We've got everything going for us," she said briskly, as if she were trying not to think about Wonder Woman. "Brains, experience . . ." She swung her leg over the seat and pushed off into the street.

"How about clues? What about leads?" I reminded her as I hopped onto my bike and headed out into the street after her. "We don't have any of them. And where are we going anyway?" I shouted, putting on an extra burst of speed. (My bike's a ten-speed, brand-new

33

last Christmas, but it doesn't seem to make much difference when it comes to keeping up with P.J. Clover!)

P.J. slowed down. And for a moment, it looked as if she didn't know where we were going. As if she were pedaling just to get away from the scene of her one-sided bet! But as I drew up alongside her, she recovered herself quickly and replied, "To the clubhouse, of course. We're going to go through your notes. Sift them for evidence. Search them for clues. There's something strange going on in that jewelry store," she said seriously. "Something peculiar about the way Mr. Findletter was acting. Why didn't he want the police to investigate, for instance? Why did he act so upset when he heard we were trying to help? And what was so special about that necklace anyway? If we could figure out a few things like that, we'd be on our way to catching that redheaded—"

"So! You really *don't* think Annalise did it," I interrupted.

"No," P.J. admitted, looking a bit sheepish. "Not unless she's an awfully good liar. But I couldn't let Butch get away with thinking he had it all figured out, could I? And we do have to consider every possibility." She swerved to avoid hitting a car that was parked in the bike lane. "And besides, it is pretty strange that the thief just vanished into thin air!"

"But P.J.," I said, swerving my bike around the parked car, too. "She probably had a getaway car waiting." Thieves in movies always had getaway cars. "She probably stepped right out of the store, hopped into her car, and—"

Drove off into the sunset, I was going to say. Or maybe to Idaho, or Colorado, or Alaska, even. (In which

34

case we'd never find her—unless P.J. was planning to trade in our bikes for dogsleds!)

That's what I was going to say.

But P.J. didn't give me a chance. Instead, she suddenly slammed on her brakes and skidded to a halt right in the middle of the bike lane. "Stacy!" she exclaimed. "That's it! We *do* have a lead!"

"We do?" I stopped beside her. I didn't know what she was talking about.

"Don't you remember?" she said, her nose giving an impatient twitch. "Mrs. Bigelow—Butch's very own mother—said that the street in front of Findletter's was closed for repairs yesterday. Well, if the street was closed, then there *couldn't* have been a getaway car. And if there wasn't a getaway car, then the thief must have walked away from the shop. And if she walked away, someone *must* have seen her. No one could stroll through downtown Mill Creek dressed the way she was and *not* be noticed!"

She was right about that. Mill Creek goes in for jeans and jogging shoes, not rhinestone-studded sunglasses and long white gloves. "But the police searched," I pointed out. "They must have asked people if they'd seen her."

But P.J. dismissed the Mill Creek police force with an impatient wave of her hand. "They couldn't have talked to everyone," she said. "And they probably didn't even bother to ask little kids. Now, if we could just reach some of those people . . . All we need is one witness, after all. Just one person who saw her. That would prove that the robbery really happened, that Annalise Brown didn't make the whole thing up!"

She was right, of course, but she was forgetting one

35

thing. "P.J., you bet Butch that we'd find the *necklace* by Saturday. Just finding a witness isn't going to . . ."

But P.J. dismissed my objections with another impatient wave of her hand. "What's a bet compared to a person's life," she said nobly. "And besides, if we find a witness, we'll be on our way to finding the thief. And if we find the thief, we'll find the necklace. We'll be helping Annalise at the same time we're helping ourselves. To say nothing of showing Mr. Findletter that we're *not* playing games!"

She made it all sound so simple. "But how are we going to do it?" I said. "There's no time to put an ad in the *Gazette.*" I was thinking of something like: *Whoever saw a redheaded thief come out of Findletter's Jewelry Store on Wednesday afternoon, call 388-9456* (that's our phone number) *immediately!* "Even if we flew to the newspaper office, we'd—"

"Wait a second," P.J. interrupted. "Say that again."

"Say what?"

" 'Even if we flew,' " she repeated, her eyes lighting up. "Well, that's it. That's what we'll do. We'll make flyers!"

It took a moment for my mind to make the leap from flying to the newspaper office to the kind of flyers P.J. Clover was talking about. Then it dawned on me. "You mean flyers like the ones we put up around town to advertise our dog-walking business?" I pictured the signs—bright yellow paper with a drawing (made by me, of course)—of two girls walking a dog.

"Exactly!" P.J. said. "Only this time we won't be advertising for dogs." She gripped the handlebars of her bike, pushed off, and began to pedal again—fast.

36

"We'll be advertising for a thief! Or at any rate, for someone who *saw* a thief!"

"But P.J.—" I was going to say that putting up a bunch of signs didn't mean that the thief was going to fall into our laps. I was going to point out that time was short. But P.J. was already too far ahead of me to hear. All I could do was hop back on my bike and speed after her. Down Miller, onto Sycamore, around the corner and onto our block. Even though I was pedaling as fast as I could, I didn't catch up with her until we reached the Clovers' driveway.

"I know we've got some of that yellow paper left," P.J. said, scarcely out of breath as she dumped her bike and headed in the direction of the backyard. It'll be perfect. We'll write on it with red marking pens. Or maybe we'll have copies made at The Copy Shop. That way we could put up fifty . . . a hundred . . ."

She sounded so enthusiastic that I didn't have the heart to point out what a long shot it was. After all, if I were about to lose something important—like a T-shirt collection—I might be grasping at straws too!

I parked my bike—you don't dump an almost brand-new ten-speed!—and headed after her as she disappeared around the corner of the garage. "We'll have this case solved in no time," she was saying. "Butch Bigelow's going to be sorry he ever . . ."

Suddenly she stopped. "You!" she exclaimed.

I came around the corner of the garage just in time to see a girl dressed in blue overalls dotted with red strawberries jump up from our clubhouse steps.

"What are you doing here?" P.J. said as Tina Toomey

marched across the yard in our direction. "I already told you we don't have time—"

"Oh, yes, you do!"

The husky voice echoed across the yard as its owner, a tall, stocky, brown-haired boy, stepped out from behind the clubhouse. He was followed by another tall, stocky, brown-haired boy. The two looked exactly alike because that's what they were—identical. Tina Toomey's identical twin brothers, Dick and Tuck, better known in the neighborhood as the terrible Toomey twins!

"Uh-oh," I whispered, taking a step back. "Now we're in for it."

P.J. turned a shade paler, but she held her ground.

"What took you so long?" Tina said accusingly. "Butch Bigelow said you'd be right back."

"Butch Bigelow?" The color returned to P.J.'s cheeks. "What does he have to do with this?"

"*He's* my friend," Tina replied, coming to a halt in front of us. "*He* said you'd find my baby. I was outside his house when he came home for his violin lesson, and when I told him about how you wouldn't help, he said he was sure that if I brought my brothers with me you'd change your mind."

"Oh, no," P.J. groaned. "The skunk. The dirty, low-down—"

But before she could finish her description of Butch Bigelow, the terrible Toomeys advanced across the yard.

"Now . . . now wait a second," P.J. said nervously as they backed us into the driveway. "Maybe we can work something out. We can't get to it right away, but maybe later . . ."

"No," said Dick, towering over us.

There aren't many kids in Park School who can tower over P.J. Clover, but the Toomey twins can.

"Not later," said Tuck.

"Now!"

The twins moved closer together, and suddenly we were facing a solid wall of Toomeys! "You're going to find that doll of hers by noon on Saturday or . . ."

"By Saturday?" P.J. repeated. "Noon? But we can't do that. We've got an important case to solve. We can't—"

"Oh, yes, you can," Dick interrupted. "Because if you don't, *we're* not going to be able to go on our camping trip!"

"She'll refuse to get in the car," explained Tuck, jerking his thumb in Tina's direction.

"She'll roll on the ground and hold her breath until she turns blue in the face," said Dick.

"It's true," Tina put in. "I won't *want* to, but I'll have to. I won't be able to help myself."

"And then the whole family will have to stay home," concluded Dick. "Get the picture?"

P.J. and I exchanged a glance. We got it, all right. Though it certainly wasn't a pretty one.

"Well, I guess we could try," I said meekly.

"You'd better do more than just try," Tuck warned.

"Right," Dick said, scowling fiercely. "Because if you don't find it, something bad could happen." His eyes fell on my almost brand-new ten-speed. "Something *bad* like a bent wheel."

"Or a slashed tire," Tuck said.

"Or a broken frame."

"Or—"

39

"You wouldn't dare!" P.J. interrupted, her eyes blazing.

"Oh, yes, they would." I grabbed her arm as she took a step toward Dick and Tuck. "Don't you remember Kevin Zamorra's racer and Susie Supinski's drum set?" Kevin and Susie were just two of the poor souls who'd been foolish enough to cross the terrible Toomeys.

"They'd do it, P.J.," I warned. "They really would."

The Toomeys nodded. "We'd have to," they said solemnly.

"They'd have to," Tina agreed.

"But don't worry," said Dick. "It probably won't come to that because you're so good at finding dolls. Even Butch Bigelow says so."

I tightened my grip on P.J.'s arm, holding her back as the Toomeys began to hustle Tina down the street. "Gotta get her home," Dick called over his shoulder. "She won't eat supper if she misses 'Speed Racer.' "

"Be at our house tomorrow morning," Tuck shouted.

"I'll tell you *everything* then," Tina promised. "I know that you'll find her."

"By Saturday!" Dick said.

"At noon," Tuck added, as the gruesome trio disappeared around the corner. "You'll find her by then, or else!"

I stared at my bike. At the bright blue paint with hardly a chip, at the shiny chrome I'd so lovingly polished. "What are we going to do?" I said desperately, turning to P.J.

"Don't worry," she replied quickly. "Those creeps aren't going to lay a finger on your bike."

"But what about your T-shirts? What about An-

41

nalise? If we don't find that necklace by Saturday, you'll . . . she'll . . ."

P.J. looked grim.

I held my breath. What was she going to say? That we'd have to give up on the necklace, give up on the T-shirts? Or was she thinking about my bike? Was she thinking that it would have to be sacrificed? But no. None of those awful possibilities was going through P.J. Clover's mind.

"There's only thing we *can* do," she said. "Find them *both*!"

5

Stolen!

One difference between P.J. Clover and me (as you may have noticed) is that *she* thinks anything's possible, whereas *I* have my doubts. I was having them—plenty of them—right now.

"But do you really think we can do it?" I said anxiously.

For a moment, *just* for a moment, P.J. hesitated and I thought I saw a flicker of doubt in her eyes. But then . . . "Of course we can!" she said. "Finding that doll won't take any time at all. We'll just go over to Tina's house tomorrow morning before school. It's probably stuck behind the sofa or buried under a pile of junk. It'll be easy to dig it out."

"But it might not be," I warned. I'd been in the Toomeys' house. It struck me as a place where things could disappear and never be seen again. "And Saturday's just two days away. I don't see how we can—"

"Well, we *will*," P.J. interrupted. This time she sounded as if she were trying to convince herself just as much as me. "We're not going to let Butch Bigelow get away with this. He's going to be sorry he ever sent Tina and her dumb brothers over here!"

"But P.J.—" I began.

"No more buts," she commanded. "Now come on. If we're going to solve two cases in two days, we don't have any time to lose. We'll start by making those flyers." She grabbed me by the arm and dragged me across the backyard toward the clubhouse. "Then we'll read through your notes, and then—"

But before she could say what we'd do next, she was stopped by a voice calling from across the backyard.

"Oh, there you are!" It was Mrs. Clover. She was leaning out the kitchen window. "Your mother just called, Stacy," she said. "She wants you to come home right away. Something about a room you were supposed to clean."

I groaned. How could I clean my room at a time like this? Nancy Drew never had to clean her room. Neither did Sherlock Holmes.

"Don't worry," P.J. said, as if she could read my mind. "I'll take care of the flyers. I'll copy them at The Copy Shop. We can afford it. We've got money in the treasury."

That money had come from a bet with Butch that P.J. *had* won!

"I'll get lots made," she went on, "and we'll meet at the Toomeys' house tomorrow at eight. That'll give us plenty of time to find Tina's old doll. And meanwhile . . ." She paused, the expression on her face serious. "Meanwhile, I'm going to see what I can find out about Mr. Findletter. There's something peculiar about the way he—"

44

But again, Mrs. Clover interrupted. "P.J., you'd better let Stacy go," she warned. "Her mother sounded like she meant business."

That made me move. Because, now that I thought of it, my room had been on my mother's mind—though not on *mine*—for more than a week.

"Don't worry," P.J. called as I hurried back toward the driveway. "It'll work out. You'll see. The Toomeys won't get anywhere near your bike, but . . ." She hesitated. "But just in case . . ." She looked embarrassed.

"Just in case what?" I said suspiciously.

"Well, maybe you'd better put it somewhere safe," she replied quickly. "Like in a cellar. With the chain on. And the door locked!"

That advice certainly didn't do much for my peace of mind. Especially since my house doesn't have a cellar! I had to be content with parking my bike in the garage as usual and double-checking to make sure that the door was locked.

It didn't help, either, when at dinner my brother, Victor, told a hair-raising story about a wrestling match he'd witnessed between the Toomeys and Kurt Hoffmann, the biggest bully at school. "Dick and Tuck took turns, and each one got him pinned down just like that," Victor said, snapping his fingers. "Those guys are *strong,* I tell you. Why, they could probably bend a bicycle just like a piece of licorice!"

I nearly choked on my chicken. And I hardly noticed the story my mother, who works in the attendance office at the high school where P.J.'s mother teaches, told about a girl named Finella who wanted to drop out of school and go to New York to become an actress. I certainly didn't pay much attention to my father's account of his day at work. And I might not even have been able to finish dinner if we hadn't been having apple pie for dessert!

I tried to tell myself that other people had problems, too. After all, Annalise might be hauled off to jail. (Would she be able to get a job as a counselor at camp if she had a police record? I wondered.) P.J. might lose her T-shirts—Wonder Woman, Mickey Mouse, the Carlsbad Caverns, all of them. But thinking about that didn't make me feel any better. It made me feel worse.

By the time I arrived at the Toomeys' house the next morning, I was convinced that this time P.J. Clover was wrong. We'd *never* be able to solve two cases in two days. Especially when one of them was a real crime that I wasn't even sure—in spite of wanting to help Annalise—we should be mixed up in. And we certainly wouldn't find Tina's doll before school. The tardy bell would ring in just forty-five minutes. Our other lost doll cases—even the easy ones—had taken a lot longer to solve than that!

I looked anxiously up and down the block. P.J. wasn't usually late, especially when we were on a case. But maybe, in spite of what she'd said, she wasn't eager to waste time on a doll. Maybe she'd thought about it last night and decided that my bike wasn't worth trying to save.

But then, before I could think any more nervous thoughts about P.J., she came racing around the corner on her battered old three-speed. Her bookbag was slung over one shoulder, a bunch of papers sticking out the top. Her hair was tangled, as if she'd barely had time to run a comb through it, and she was wearing a T-shirt that looked brand-new. It was bright orange, and across the front in big white letters were the words *Never Underestimate the Power of a Woman!*

"Bought it last night," she announced, as she screeched to a halt, leaped from her bike—I'd left mine home in the garage, of course—and bounded across the Toomeys' front lawn. "Like it?" she asked.

I stared at the shirt. I liked it all right, but the only good thing I could say about it right now was that Butch Bigelow wouldn't!

"Are you nuts, P.J.?" I exclaimed. "Buying a new T-shirt at a time like this? Don't you realize you could lose it—you could lose them all—tomorrow?"

P.J. looked as if she'd been waiting for me to say exactly what I'd said. "Wrong!" she declared. She pulled a wrinkled sheet of paper from her bookbag and held it out to me. I could see she was excited, but what the paper, which looked like some kind of advertising flyer, could have to do with it, I couldn't imagine.

I reached out to take it from her hand, but just then the Toomeys' front door opened and a harried-looking woman burst out. It was Mrs. Toomey. She was dressed in a business suit, with a diaper pin stuck in one lapel and a lump of Pablum clinging to the other.

"Late for work," she explained, rushing down the steps as if she couldn't wait to put some distance between herself and the house. The sound of a baby's crying came from inside. "You're not looking for Dick and Tuck, are you?" she asked doubtfully.

"No," P.J. replied. (I wondered if anyone ever came looking for Dick and Tuck!) "We're looking for Tina. We're here to find—"

47

"Oh, but of course!" Mrs. Toomey exclaimed. "The doll!" A grateful look came over her face. "The twins said you'd volunteered to help."

"Volunteered?" I echoed, forgetting about P.J.'s mysterious paper, forgetting about everything, in fact, except the terrible Toomeys and the threats they'd made to my bike. "Is that what they told you?"

But Mrs. Toomey wasn't listening. She was already halfway to her car. "Go on in," she called over her shoulder. "Tina's in the kitchen. They're *all* in the kitchen."

P.J. stuffed the paper she'd been about to show me back into her bookbag. "This can wait," she said, heading for the door. "We'll get this doll business out of the way. Then we can concentrate on more important stuff!"

I refrained from saying that my bike *was* important stuff—this was no time to argue after all—and hurried down the Toomeys' front hall after P.J.

The kitchen wasn't hard to find. All we had to do was follow the scent of burning toast. When we got there, Mr. Toomey was scraping a piece into the sink, the Toomey toddler—whose name I couldn't remember—was crawling around at his feet, and the latest Toomey baby—whose name I couldn't remember, either—was sitting in a high chair spitting Pablum at anyone who came within range.

Tina was at the table, toying with a bowl of Cocoa Puffs. "You came!" she cried when she saw us. She leaped up from the table, knocking over a glass of milk. "You're going to find her. You're going to find my Baby Cuddles!"

Mr. Toomey grabbed a sponge from the sink. He took a quick glance at P.J.'s T-shirt before bending down to mop up the milk. "Terrific," he said. "We could use some kind of power around here." He straightened up and shoved another spoonful of Pablum into the baby's mouth. "But I hope you can find it fast, girls," he added as the toddler started banging a couple of pot lids together. "We're supposed to go c-a-m-p—"

He started to spell out *camping*, but Tina was too smart for that.

"I will *not* go without my baby!" she said, stamping her foot.

The toddler banged the pot lids together again.

Mr. Toomey made a quick trade—the lids for the piece of scraped toast—and turned to Tina. "That's enough," he warned. "Now, just tell these girls what happened and be quick about it. They've got to get to school."

"Right," P.J. agreed. "In fact, we'd better get started right away. You take the living room, Stacy. Check behind the sofa. And I'll go through the clothes hamper."

"The clothes hamper?" Mr. Toomey looked confused.

"That's right," P.J. said, already on her way out of the kitchen. "We've found lots of lost dolls in—"

"Don't call her a doll!" Tina shouted, stamping her foot again. "She is *not* a doll, she's a *baby*. And she's not *lost!*"

"Not lost?" For a fleeting moment I thought we were saved. "But I thought you said—"

"I did not," Tina interrupted indignantly. "I would *never* lose my Baby Cuddles. She's not lost, she's—"

"Stolen," Mr. Toomey put in quickly. "I thought you

50

girls knew that. She was stolen right out of her carriage."

P.J. stopped dead in her tracks.

I felt my heart sink. Lost was one thing, but stolen . . . A vision of my shiny blue bike, its body all mangled and twisted, leaped into my mind.

"Are you sure?" P.J. turned on Tina. "Are you absolutely sure? You don't think you could have . . . ?"

"Of course, I'm sure," Tina replied, her lower lip beginning to tremble, her eyes filling with tears. "Don't you think I know what happened to my very own baby?"

"Now, Tina," Mr. Toomey said nervously. "Don't get upset. Just tell these girls what happened as it happened. Then they can try to figure out where your doll—I mean"—he caught himself just in time—"I mean, your baby, is. Doesn't that sound like a good plan?"

"It sounds like the *only* plan," I muttered. "Aside from wringing Butch Bigelow's neck!"

P.J. looked as if she agreed (about Butch's neck, that is), but she didn't waste time on wishful thinking. Instead, she shot a quick glance at the clock above the sink—just twenty-five minutes before school would begin—and got down to business.

"All right, Tina," she said, starting to pace back and forth in the crowded kitchen. "We don't have much time, so let's get the facts straight. Your doll—I mean, your baby—was stolen from her carriage. Now, *when* was she stolen?"

Tina struggled to pull herself together. "The . . . the day before yesterday." She sniffed and sat back down in her chair.

I pulled my notebook from my pocket and flipped to a clean page, beyond all the pages and pages of notes I'd taken at Findletter's Jewelry Store yesterday. I wrote down the name of the victim, Baby Cuddles, and the date of the crime, Wednesday, October 19th.

"And what time was it—I mean, she—stolen?" P.J. went on.

The toddler, who'd taken to pacing along behind her, blew a shower of toast crumbs from his mouth and giggled.

"Around three o'clock," replied Tina, giving her brother a poke that sent him yowling to his father. He latched onto Mr. Toomey's leg as if it were a raft in a storm.

I wrote down the words, around three o'clock. I felt as if I'd written them before. Combined with the date that I'd just jotted down, there was something familiar about them.

"Mommy and I were—"

"Buying bugs," Mr. Toomey interrupted, as if he wanted to hurry things along. "For the twins' tarantula." He picked up the baby—who was beginning to have a disagreeable smell about her—and pried the toddler loose from his leg. "It was my wife's day to stay home with the kids," he explained, sounding as if he wished every day were his wife's day! "They went to the pet shop to get crickets—that's what the tarantula eats—and Tina put the doll—I mean, the *baby* carriage in the passageway between Findletter's and—"

"Findletter's?" P.J. said. She stopped pacing.

"That's right," Mr. Toomey replied. "There's a passageway right there between the pet shop and—"

52

But P.J. didn't give him a chance to finish. "Wait a second!" she said. "Do you mean to say that Tina's doll was taken from a carriage parked between Findletter's and the pet shop the day before yesterday at around three? But that's when—"

"The jewelry store was robbed!" Tina leaped up from her chair again, this time knocking over the box of Cocoa Puffs. "But I didn't know it would be. If I'd known, I never would have left her there. I never would have. . . ."

"Stacy, did you hear that?" P.J. exclaimed, ignoring Tina's blubbering. "She was there. She was actually there!" She turned on Tina, grabbing her by the shoulders, and giving her a shake. "What did you see?" she demanded. "Did you see anyone come out? Did you see a redheaded—"

"Let go!" Tina cried, squirming out of her grip. "I didn't see anyone. I didn't see anything. I already told the police that. I told them about my baby, too, but they didn't care. They didn't care about anything but that stupid old robbery."

"Now, Tina, the police had a lot on their minds," Mr. Toomey put in. "I understand it was pretty chaotic," he said to us. "The burglar alarm was ringing and people were coming out of the stores. Everyone was looking for this redheaded—"

"Well, they'd better find her!" Tina interrupted. "*You'd* better find her," she said, turning to P.J. and me. "You'd better find her, because *she's* the one who took my Baby Cuddles!"

6

Serious Stuff

For a moment, P.J. and I were too surprised to speak. The jewel thief, a doll thief?

I was having a hard enough time adjusting to the idea of two crimes—two crimes that *we* were trying to solve—being committed in the same place at the same time. To suggest that they were both carried out by the same person was too much for me!

I could see that P.J., in spite of her *Trust no one . . . suspect everyone* rule, was having a hard time believing it, too. "But how could that be?" she said. "You just told us you didn't see anyone, so how do you know—"

"She doesn't," Mr. Toomey interrupted. "It's just an idea she's gotten into her head. Obviously, this redheaded woman—whoever she was—didn't take Baby Cuddles."

"Oh, yes, she did," Tina insisted. "She was a thief. She was there. If she was stealing jewelry, why wouldn't she steal my baby? My Baby Cuddles is worth a lot more than any old necklace!"

"To you, Tina." Mr. Toomey sighed, as if he'd been over all this before. "She was valuable to *you*, but not necessarily to anyone else."

Tina was not convinced. "Well, if she didn't take her," she said, putting her hands on her hips and looking squarely at her father, P.J., and me, "who did?"

It was another conversation stopper. And this time, not even P.J. Clover had an answer. I saw her glance quickly at the clock. It was a bad sign. P.J. doesn't care about being late for school when she's doing things she thinks are important, but when she thinks she's just wasting her time . . .

"How about a note?" I suggested desperately, grasping at straws. "If someone knew how much Baby Cuddles was worth to Tina, they might have taken her and left a note. For ransom, I mean."

Tina turned pale at the thought.

Mr. Toomey shook his head. "Afraid not," he said. "But if you want to check the carriage, you can." He shifted the baby to his other arm, stepped into the utility room, and returned a moment later wheeling a white wicker doll carriage in front of him.

At the sight of it, Tina burst into tears. "My baby," she said, sobbing as P.J. (remembering, perhaps, that our business cards *did* say "No case too small") started to dig through the pillows and blankets inside. "My poor baby. She—or whoever it was—took her new pink blanket and Mommy's scarf that was in the carriage, but . . . but they didn't take my baby's food. Without her food, she'll . . . she'll starve!"

55

A vision of the food Baby Cuddles eats—a gloopy gelatin mixture that you shove in one end and it comes out the other, yuk!—popped into my mind. "Now, Tina," I began, "you know she won't really . . ." But the look on Tina's face told me I was treading on dangerous ground. "I mean, she'll just get a little bit hungry. Isn't that right, P.J.?"

But P.J. wasn't thinking about Baby Cuddles' stomach. She was busy shaking the contents of the carriage—the mattress, blankets, and pillows—over the kitchen floor. I held my breath, hoping for something that would give us a lead. But nothing—no rings, no buttons, no keys, no mysterious scraps of paper or locks of hair—fell out. Whoever had taken Baby Cuddles had left without a trace.

"I guess we could check the passageway outside the pet store," P.J. said, stuffing the bedding back into the carriage. "There might be footprints or . . ." Then she stopped and I could see by the look on her face that she must have remembered that the passageway outside the pet store was paved in cement!

"You see the problem," said Mr. Toomey. "No note, no clues, nothing. My wife and I haven't known what to do. In fact, the only thing we could think of was making these." He took a stack of papers from the top of the refrigerator. "They're flyers."

"Flyers?" P.J.'s nose gave a sudden twitch.

"That's right," Mr. Toomey said. "Flyers asking if anyone saw Tina's doll being taken out of her carriage on Wednesday afternoon. Given the circumstances, it seemed the only way we'd ever find her. We made them last night, but unfortunately we haven't had a chance to put them up. Then, when the twins said you were willing to help, we thought that maybe you could do it."

He didn't have to ask twice.

P.J., her eyes shining, snatched the flyers from his hand. "Brilliant idea!" she exclaimed, stuffing the flyers into her bookbag along with the ones advertising for the redheaded thief. I wasn't sure what was going through her mind, but whatever it was, it made the discouraged look that had come over her face as she searched the carriage completely disappear.

"Stacy, this is perfect," she whispered, turning to me. "Exactly what we need to—"

"It is *not* polite to whisper!" Tina interrupted, stamping her foot again. "You're supposed to be figuring out how to get my baby back. And Mommy's scarf, too. You can't forget that because it was her favorite. It had little flowers and birds and . . ."

But P.J. wasn't interested in the flowers and birds on Mrs. Toomcy's scarf. In fact, she wasn't even listening to what Tina was saying. She was already heading for the door. "Don't worry about a thing," she told Mr. Toomey, who looked relieved to have passed at least part of his job on to us. "We'll have the town plastered with these by this afternoon. Whoever took Baby Cuddles isn't going to get away with it. And neither is Butch Bigelow!" she added, grabbing me by the arm. "Come on," she commanded. "We've got work to do!"

"But, P.J., don't you think we should . . ." I began. Then I stopped. Because what else was there for us to do? We'd found out where and when Tina's doll had been taken. Tina and her father had told us everything they knew. Now it was up to us—if we wanted to save my bike, that is—to find her!

"My wife and I really appreciate this," Mr. Toomey called as P.J. hustled me out the kitchen door. The baby cooed and the toddler picked up the pot lids and banged them together again.

I saw Tina wipe her eyes and blow her nose on the edge of the tablecloth. "I appreciate it too," she yelled as P.J. and I hurried down the hall. "If you find my baby, I will be your best friend forever!"

Which made me think, just for a moment, that in spite of my bike, finding Baby Cuddles might not be such a good thing to do!

P.J. bounded down the Toomeys' front steps. "Can you believe it?" she said, grabbing her bike from where she'd dumped it on the front lawn. "This is perfect!" She swung one of her long, skinny legs over the seat and motioned for me to hop on behind.

I did. I knew I wasn't supposed to be riding on the back of anyone's bike, of course—too dangerous, my mother said—but this was an emergency.

"But P.J.—" I began, hanging on tight as she turned the bike into the street and began to pedal furiously in the direction of school. "I don't see anything so perfect about it. We still have to find Tina's doll. We still have to find the necklace. We still have to solve two cases."

"But that's just it," P.J. said, whizzing around the corner onto Sycamore. "Don't you see? With two sets of flyers, we double our odds. Think of it. Both robberies took place in the same spot at the same time. That means that anyone who saw the doll thief might have seen the jewel thief, and anyone who saw the jewel thief might have seen the doll thief. Butch Bigelow's going to kick himself when he finds out how his dumb scheme turned out. Instead of making things harder, he's made things easier. He's given us a chance to solve two—no, *three*—cases at one blow!"

"Three? What do you mean by three?" I said as we raced up the block toward Park School. "I only count two. The doll and the—"

"That's because you don't know what I found out last night!" P.J. made a sharp turn into the schoolyard and skidded to a halt in front of the bike rack. She shoved the bike into a slot, barely giving me a chance to hop off behind, and pulled her bookbag from her shoulder. "It's proof," she said, starting to rummage through the papers inside. "Proof of what I was trying to figure out in the jewelry store yesterday. Proof that Mr. Findletter—"

But before she could finish her sentence, she was interrupted by a shout from across the schoolyard.

"Clover! Hey, Clover!"

It was Butch Bigelow! He was making his way toward us through the crowd of kids flooding into the school building. He had a camera—the kind that develops pictures on the spot—hanging from a strap around his neck and a paperback book in his hand. As he drew nearer I could see the picture on the cover—a painting of a man with a knife sticking out of his back, lying in a pool of shiny red blood!

P.J. quickly stopped rummaging and zipped up her bookbag. "Now what does he—" she began.

But Butch was already upon us.

"It's over, Clover!" he announced triumphantly, the freckles practically popping off his nose. "You can pack up your shirts. You can—" He stopped as he noticed the words on P.J.'s new orange T-shirt. "Except for

59

that one," he said quickly, wrinkling up his nose in disgust. "You can keep *that*, but I'll take the rest. Because I've got this case solved!"

"You what?" P.J.'s face turned pale and her hand went up to her chest. She stared at Butch as if he'd just said he could spin straw into gold. "What do you mean?" she said. "How could you possibly have anything solved?"

"Easy," Butch replied smugly. "It's all in here!"

He waved the paperback book in our faces, and suddenly, I recognized the name of the author, C.D. Forrester—Butch's aunt who lives in New Jersey and writes detective books.

P.J. recognized the name, too. And as she did, some of the color that had drained from her cheeks when Butch made his announcement, returned. "Do you mean to tell us," she said, "that you think you have this case solved just because of something you read in one of your aunt's books?"

Butch bristled. "Well, why not?" he replied. "She knows a lot about crime. And the case in this book is a lot like—"

"But how about the necklace?" I interrupted, suddenly angry, suddenly remembering that if it wasn't for Butch, we wouldn't be chasing after Tina's doll, if it wasn't for Butch, my bike would be safe. "Did you find that? Did you find the redheaded thief?"

Butch squirmed. The smug expression that had decorated his face a moment before faded. "Well . . . not quite," he admitted. "Not yet, but . . ."

"Then you *don't* have the case solved," declared P.J., the rest of the color coming back to her cheeks as the tardy bell began to ring.

60

"But I've got it figured out," Butch protested, running after us as we made a dash for the school building. "See, in this book, there's a robbery. Only it's not really a robbery. Because the thing that was stolen was already stolen. That's why the guy it was stolen from didn't want the police to . . ."

P.J. suddenly stopped.

We were just outside our classroom. The bell was still sounding, but everyone else was already seated.

"P.J., come on," I urged. "Forget about him. He doesn't know what he's talking about. We don't want Mr. Collins to mark us tardy again."

P.J. paid no attention. She was staring at Butch, a peculiar expression on her face. "Do you mean," she said, "that all that's in your aunt's book?"

"All that and more," Butch replied eagerly, seeming to forget, at least for the moment, that he and P.J. were enemies. "You see, the thing that was stolen was a bracelet. An antique bracelet. But it wasn't stolen because it was old, it was stolen because it was filled with illegal drugs. The beads were hollow and the drugs were inside. And the guy it was stolen from wasn't an antique dealer like he said he was. He was a drug dealer. The guy who stole it was part of a rival drug ring, and—"

"Wait a second," I interrupted, forgetting about being tardy, forgetting about everything except the incredible suggestion that Butch seemed to be making. "Are you saying that Mr. Findletter . . . ?"

"I'm saying it," Butch replied grimly, "and I'm proving it. That's what this is for." He put his hand on the camera hanging around his neck. "This is serious stuff," he said earnestly. "If we're going to crack this thing, we'll—I mean, I'll—need hard evidence. Something that will stand up in court. Pictures, maybe tapes . . ."

But before he could list every crime-busting device he'd ever seen on TV, the tardy bell stopped ringing. The kids inside the classroom started opening their desks, getting out pencils, rustling papers. There was no time to lose. The moment Mr. Collins turned his back, all three of us ducked through the door and slipped into our seats.

I was still in a state of shock at what Butch had said, or almost said. Mr. Findletter—mild-mannered Mr. Findletter, respected businessman, president of the Chamber of Commerce, sponsor of a Little League team—a drug dealer? There was no way it could be true.

"Isn't that the craziest thing you ever heard?" I whispered, leaning across the aisle toward P.J.

She'd been silent ever since Butch had given his synopsis of his aunt's book. Now she glanced quickly in Butch's direction and slid across the seat toward me. "It would be," she whispered back, "except for one thing."

I looked at her curiously. "What's that?"

"He's right," she replied solemnly. "This time, Butch Bigelow is right!"

7

Lapis Lazuli

Right?

I opened my mouth to speak—not sure what I was going to say—but just then Mr. Collins turned around. He frowned in our direction.

P.J. slid back into her seat like a turtle withdrawing into its shell. "Recess," she hissed as she went. "The girls' lavatory. I'll show you then!"

And that was that. No time for questions. No time for anything, in fact, except listening to Mr. Collins make the morning announcements. There was a whole list of things. Lunch money would be due Monday. A drama group from the high school was going to entertain us after recess. It was time to begin thinking about science fair projects. But none of it meant anything to me, because all I could think of was Butch. All I could think of was what he'd said about Mr. Findletter. But it couldn't be true. No matter how nasty Mr. Findletter had been to P.J. and me, no matter how meanly he was treating Annalise, he would never be involved in . . .

"Drugs?" P.J.'s voice echoed off the tile walls. The recess bell had finally rung and we were in the girls' lavatory at last. "Of course not, Stacy," she said, a shocked expression on her face. "Mr. Findletter would never . . ."

"But, P.J.," I objected, "you said—"

"I said that Butch was right, but not about"—she lowered her voice even though we were the only ones in the lavatory—"not about drugs. No, Stacy, it was the first part of what he said—the part about the thing that was stolen already being stolen. That's what I think he was right about. Look."

She unzipped her bookbag, which she'd carried into the lavatory with her, and whipped out the wrinkled-up sheet of paper she'd been trying to show me all morning. "I found this last night in The Copy Shop, in a box of stuff people had left behind in the machine."

She thrust the paper, which looked like this

STOLEN NECKLACE

Lapis lazuli and gold
Family heirloom
SUBSTANTIAL REWARD FOR ITS RETURN
NO QUESTIONS ASKED
Phone 555–0394

into my hand. "See that," she said, pointing to the words beneath the picture. "Lapis lazuli. That's a deep blue mineral composed mainly of lazurite, used chiefly as a gem or as a pigment. I looked it up in the dictionary. And the beads in between are gold, and it's a family heirloom so it must be old. . . . Don't you see, Stacy? *This* necklace is the *same* necklace that was stolen from Findletter's Jewelry Store!"

So that was it! I stared at the flyer I held in my hand. Now that I knew what lapis lazuli was, I could see that the necklace in the picture could easily be the one that Annalise Brown had described. It even had a catch in the shape of a dolphin. And yet . . . "I don't get it," I said, feeling confused. "If this necklace was stolen, then how did it get into—"

"Easy," P.J. replied before I could finish my sentence. "Mr. Findletter bought it. Don't you remember? Annalise said the necklace wasn't priced because Mr. Findletter had just bought it—'from a man who's been coming in lately to sell him things.' Those were her exact words. Well, I think that man was—"

"A thief!" I exclaimed, suddenly seeing what she was getting at. "You mean you think the guy who stole this necklace brought it into the jewelry store and tricked Mr. Findletter into buying it!" It was easy, now that I thought of it, to see how it could have happened. The thief probably told some sort of sob story about having to sell the family jewels and Mr. Findletter felt sorry for him, so . . .

But P.J. was shaking her head.

"No, Stacy, that's not what I mean," she said. "What I mean is that Mr. Findletter bought the necklace *knowing* it was stolen. That's what I was trying to think of in the jewelry store yesterday. That's why I said we've got *three* crimes to solve. Don't you see, Stacy? Mr. Findletter is a fence!"

For a moment, I didn't know what she was talking about. White picket? Redwood board? Chain link? Then it hit me. The kind of fence P.J. meant was the kind of fence you see in crime shows on TV—someone who buys stolen goods from thieves and sells them for a big profit. It's not as bad as being a drug dealer—nothing is *that* bad—but . . . "I don't believe it, P.J.," I said. "Mr. Findletter would never—"

"Then why didn't he want the police to look for the necklace?" she countered. "Why didn't he want *us* to investigate? And besides," she went on before I could even begin to think of an answer, "he's got the perfect motivation—money. 'The root of all evil,' " she quoted from somewhere. "Remember how Annalise said she wanted to make a big sale because Mr. Findletter was worried about—"

"But, P.J.," I objected. Now she was really going too far! "Lots of people worry about money. That doesn't mean they're thieves. Just think of who Mr. Findletter is. The president of the Chamber of Commerce. Sponsor of a Little League team. It would be crazy for him to—"

"But *that* may be exactly it!"

P.J. had a crazy sort of gleam in her eye, but I could see she was serious. Dead serious. "Listen," she said, lowering her voice again, though we were still the only ones in the lavatory. "I know this is hard to believe. I know it doesn't sound like anything Mr. Findletter would do. But another thing I found out last night is that he's been under a lot of pressure lately. My mother was talking about it at dinner. She says he's been

66

bringing up his teenage daughter alone and she's a real handful. My mom knows because she has her in one of her classes at school. Her name's Finella and . . ."

Finella? Now where had I heard . . . ? Then I remembered. *My* mother had been talking about a girl named Finella at dinner last night, too. "Does she want to drop out of school and go to New York to become an actress?"

"Exactly!" P.J. replied. "She's been trying everything she can think of to convince her father to let her go. And *that's* why I think this fence stuff is possible. Because, besides needing money, Mr. Findletter may be so confused and exhausted that he doesn't know what he's doing. He saw a chance and he took it, because he's just not himself!"

I didn't know what to say to that. What could I say? I still didn't want to believe that Mr. Findletter was a thief. And yet I'd heard that teenagers could drive their parents crazy. Maybe they could drive them into a life of crime as well!

Then I thought of something. Something important.

"P.J., suppose this *is* true," I said. "Suppose this is the necklace, and suppose Mr. Findletter bought it because he is a . . . a fence. That still doesn't help us. It doesn't tell us who the redheaded robber was or where she went or . . ."

But P.J. waved my objections away.

"That's what all these"—she patted her bookbag, stuffed with the flyers that she and the Toomeys had made—"are for. And as for not helping us, you may be wrong about that, too. Because there *could* be a connection.

"I didn't see it myself at first," she added (before I

could object to being told I was wrong again!), "but remember how Butch said that in his aunt's book the necklace—I mean, the bracelet—was stolen by someone from a rival gang and the person it was stolen from couldn't go to the police because if he did the police would find out what he was up to? Well, suppose the same thing—or almost the same thing—happened to Mr. Findletter. Suppose the necklace that he bought from the thief was stolen back by the thief. Suppose—"

"But, P.J.," I objected, "it was a man who sold the necklace and a woman who stole it, so how . . ."

"Well, she could have been his girlfriend," P.J. insisted. Now that the idea had taken hold, she was *not* about to give it up. "Or a member of his gang, or . . . or maybe . . ." Her nose gave a twitch. "Maybe it wasn't a woman at all, Stacy," she said, her eyes opening wide, her orange T-shirt seeming to glow more brightly. "Maybe it was a man in disguise!"

"A man?" Now she was really going too far. "But surely Annalise would have known if the thief was a man."

"Not necessarily. All he'd have to do is put on a dress and those crazy sunglasses, some lipstick, a bright red wig. . . ."

"But how about whiskers?" I said. "How about . . ."

But P.J. was too carried away to listen.

"I don't know why I didn't think of this before," she said, starting to pace back and forth in front of the sinks. "It would explain a lot of things. Why Annalise thought the thief seemed familiar, how he could disappear without a trace. All he'd have to do is duck in somewhere, pull off the wig and the dress and—"

68

"Walk around naked? Come on, P.J., you can't really think . . ."

But P.J. could and she did.

"Why not?" she said. "It would be a perfect way to trick the police and everyone else. He could have had his clothes stashed away somewhere near the store. He could have stuffed the dress and the wig into a shopping bag or something. I'm not saying that that's what *did* happen, Stacy, but it's possible. You've got to admit, it's possible!"

I didn't see why I had to admit any such thing. But before I could raise any more objections, P.J. stopped pacing and began outlining her plans.

"Here's what we're going to do," she said, blowing a strand of straggly blond hair out of her eyes and giving her T-shirt a tug so that *Never Underestimate the Power of a Woman!* marched straight across her chest. "The minute school's over, we're going to go to Findletter's. We'll put up flyers along the way, of course. Ours and the Toomeys', too. That way we'll have all bases covered. Then, while stupid old Butch Bigelow is chasing around with his camera looking for drug dealers, we're going to talk to Annalise Brown again. We'll have to be careful, of course. Needing that job the way she does, she may think she has to be loyal to Mr. Findletter. But we'll convince her. We'll make her see where her duty lies. Then we'll get her to positively identify this necklace. We'll ask if it could have been a man who stole it, and then—"

But before she could say what we would do next, the bell signaling the end of recess began to ring. At the same time, the lavatory door opened, and a group of teenage girls carrying dresses and wigs and boxes of makeup burst in.

"The drama group," P.J. said, wrinkling up her nose in disgust. (She preferred real life to make-believe!) "Come on, let's get out of here." She headed out into the hallway, filled with kids hurrying back to their classrooms, with me at her heels.

My mind was swimming. I hardly knew what to think. Double-crossing thieves, men dressed as women. If this was what *real* crime was like, I was ready to go back to—

"Hey, watch out!"

I looked up, but not in time to avoid colliding with a dark-haired teenager on her way into the lavatory. "Sorry," I said quickly, bending down to pick up the curly blond wig that had fallen from her hand. At the same time, she stopped to pick up the flyer that had fluttered from mine.

I heard her draw in her breath.

"You're not hurt, are you?" I said, suddenly noticing, as I handed her the wig, that her face, which was very pretty, had turned pale. I glanced down the crowded hallway. P.J. was already turning into our classroom. "I could take you to the nurse's office."

"No! No, I'm all right," she said quickly. "Just tell me, where did you—"

But before she could finish her sentence, the lavatory door swung open and one of the girls who had burst in a moment before poked her head out. Her face was half covered with makeup and a wig was pulled over her hair. "Come on, Finny," she said, grabbing the dark-haired girl by the arm. "We're onstage in fifteen minutes!"

I barely had time to snatch the flyer from the girl's hand before she disappeared into the lavatory. And before I could even begin to think about her behavior—she couldn't have been really hurt, could she? I mean, I'm strong, but not that strong!—I heard a familiar voice, no, *two* familiar voices, behind me.

"Twenty-six hours . . ."

I spun around to see the Toomeys, Dick and Tuck, towering over me.

"That's all you've got left," they warned, unsmiling, as they turned and headed for their classroom down the hall. "Twenty-six hours or else!"

8

A College Education

Everything I'd been thinking about—the dark-haired girl, the thief with a wig, P.J.'s theories—disappeared from my head at the sound of those two little words. Twenty-six hours. Was that really all the time there was left? It was more than a day, of course—two whole hours more—but . . .

"Don't worry," P.J. said, for the umpteenth time, as we sped toward town with me on the back of her bike. It was now three o'clock, school was over, and there were just twenty-*one* hours left. "We'll find her."

But I could tell she wasn't really thinking about Baby Cuddles, and she wasn't thinking about my ten-speed either. She was thinking about glory. She'd been thinking about it ever since recess had ended.

"We'll make the newspapers for sure, Stacy," she'd whispered as we sat in the back of the auditorium scribbling our phone number onto the flyers the Toomeys had made. The drama group had been performing onstage, but I didn't see the dark-haired girl, so maybe she'd been hurt after all and had gone home. "Exposing a criminal operation right in the middle of Mill Creek. Saving an innocent young girl the police suspected while the real crook went—"

"Now wait a second, P.J.," I'd interrupted. "We don't know for sure that Mr. Findletter is a fence."

But P.J. had already made up her mind.

"What other explanation could there be?" she'd said. "No," she repeated now as she swung the bike from Sycamore onto Miller. "This is it, Stacy. This has *got* to be it!"

I hung on tight as we zipped around the bus depot and headed for the center of town. I still wasn't convinced, but I knew better than to argue. When P.J.'s that sure of something, it takes more than words to change her mind. And besides, I had other things to think of. Things like, who could have taken Tina's stupid old doll anyway? Who would want her? She was ugly, in my opinion, and she smelled, too. Musty and sort of sour, the kind of odor that only a dog would—

Then, an awful thought struck me. Maybe *that* was it. Maybe a dog had stuck its head into Baby Cuddles' carriage, grabbed her in its jaws, and . . . A chill traveled down my spine. Could that be what had happened? It would certainly explain why we hadn't found any clues in the carriage. Dogs don't drop buttons or leave notes, after all. But it would also be the worst thing that could have happened. Because dogs don't read flyers. And when they're done chewing on something, they bury it. Why, at this very moment, Baby Cuddles might be lying in a shallow grave somewhere and we'd never find her.

"P.J.," I said as we screeched to a halt in front of the Mill Creek Market, "you don't think that Tina's doll—I mean, her baby—could have been . . ."

But P.J. had already leaped from the bike and was busily tacking flyers, ours and the Toomeys', to the bulletin board by the door.

I struggled to keep the bike from falling over, then pushed it into the rack outside the market. By the time I got it stowed away, P.J. was heading down the block. She stopped just long enough for me to catch up with her, and before I could say another word about Baby Cuddles, she thrust a bunch of flyers into my hand.

"Windshields," she directed. "You take one car, I'll take the next. We'll do all of them between here and Findletter's. And keep an eye out for Butch," she added. "I don't want him to find out about this until we've had a chance to go to the police!"

"The police?" I repeated. Somehow I hadn't thought of things going quite that far. "P.J., do you really think we'll have to go to the police?"

"Well, of course we will," she said. "This isn't kid stuff. It's a real crime. We'll have to go to the police station, and we'll have to convince Annalise to go with us. They've got books down there full of pictures of criminals. She'll have to look at them and identify the thief!"

I gulped. She was right, of course. If the man who sold Mr. Findletter the necklace was a professional thief, the police probably would have a record of him. And if Mr. Findletter had bought the necklace *knowing* it was stolen, then that was a crime and the police would have to be told. Still, I couldn't help remembering who Mr. Findletter was, and I couldn't help wishing that *we* didn't have to be the ones to do the telling!

P.J., of course, had no such qualms. She wasn't thinking about Mr. Findletter and his reputation. She was thinking about us and ours.

"This could be the best thing that ever happened to us, Stacy," she said, moving off down the block. "Once the word gets around, our phone will be ringing off the hook with cases to solve. We'll probably have to buy an answering machine. Maybe we'll remodel the headquarters, too. Get some new furniture and file cabinets."

"New furniture? But P.J. . . ." I hurried after her, pausing only long enough to tuck flyers beneath the windshield wipers of every car she skipped. "We can't afford to do that," I said, catching up with her just outside of Findletter's. "There's not enough money in the treasury, and I'm going to need my allowance to—" Fix my bike when the Toomeys get through with it, is what I was going to say. But P.J. didn't give me a chance.

Before I could get another word out of my mouth, she pulled the flyer she'd found in The Copy Shop from her bookbag and thrust it beneath my nose. "Not that we're in this for the money," she said quickly, "but still . . ." She pointed to the third line from the bottom. *Substantial reward for its return.* I'd seen the words before, of course, but somehow they hadn't registered.

"Substantial," P.J. said now. "That means a lot. Enough to buy an answering machine, enough to buy all the furniture and file cabinets we want. Why, if we get this necklace back, we may even be able to finance our college educations!"

76

Or . . . A thought flashed through my mind like a streak of summer lightning. "P.J., you don't suppose . . ." I began.

But P.J. had already stuffed the flyer back into her bookbag, shoved the door of Findletter's open, and disappeared inside.

I followed, suddenly full of hope. Maybe it didn't matter if Baby Cuddles was buried in a shallow grave. Maybe it didn't matter if the Toomey twins bent my bike like a piece of licorice. Because if we got that reward . . . A vision of a brand-new ten-speed sprang, sparkling, into my mind as the door swung shut behind me.

Annalise Brown, who was dusting the shelves behind the counter, turned around. And the moment that she did, I knew that something had happened. "Stacy!" she exclaimed when she saw me. Her eyes were shining. The worry that had filled them the day before was gone, and if she was surprised that we were back, she certainly wasn't letting it show. "I've got the most wonderful news," she said, looking for all the world as if yesterday and the day before hadn't even happened. "I'm going back to college!"

"College?" Baby Cuddles and the Toomeys and my ten-speed slipped, temporarily, from my mind. "But how . . . ? I mean, where . . . where did you get the money?" I blurted the words out before I realized that, of course, it was none of my business.

"Oh, I can't tell you that," Annalise replied quickly. A trace of the anxiety that had filled her eyes the day before returned. "But I've got it and I'll start next semester!"

"So you *won't* be needing this job!" P.J., who'd been

77

listening instead of talking for a change, shot me an excited glance, and I knew exactly what she was thinking. It was far better than anything we could have hoped for. Because if Annalise didn't need to work in the jewelry store, then she wouldn't need to protect Mr. Findletter. And if she didn't need to protect Mr. Findletter, then . . .

"Is he here?" P.J. whispered, leaning across the counter toward Annalise. "Mr. Findletter, I mean."

"Why . . . why no," Annalise replied.

That was all P.J. needed to hear. "Perfect!" she said, slipping the bookbag from her shoulder and pulling it open. "Because we've got some questions to ask, and since you're not going to be needing this job anymore, you don't have to be afraid. You can tell us everything you know."

"Oh, but—" Annalise began nervously.

"No buts," P.J. interrupted. "It's your duty. To truth and justice," she added. "Now tell us," she said, pulling the flyer from her bookbag and placing it on the counter. "Is this the necklace that was stolen?"

A startled gasp escaped from Annalise's lips. She stared at the flyer. "Where . . . where did you get this?" she asked.

"Then you recognize it!" P.J. exclaimed, ignoring her question. "You can identify it."

"No!" Annalise cried. "I . . . I've never seen it before in my life." A guilty flush crept over her cheeks and her voice trembled as she spoke. "And now . . . now I think you'd better leave," she said, shoving the flyer back into P.J.'s hand. "It was wrong of me to get you involved in this in the first place. Mr. Findletter was right. You shouldn't be meddling in—"

"Meddling?" P.J. stared at her as if she couldn't believe her ears.

"That's right," Annalise said. "I've told you everything I know and now I . . . I can't . . . I mean, I don't want to talk about it!"

"But," P.J. began (despite her *no buts* rule), "you can't just . . ."

But I stopped her before she could go on.

Because I could see that Annalise was really upset. I had no idea what was happening. Obviously she had recognized the necklace, but still . . . "P.J.," I said, "she says she's never seen it before."

I put my hand on her arm and tried to pull her toward the door, but she dug in her heels, and I don't think I would have gotten her out of there at all if a couple of customers hadn't come in. They started talking to Annalise about pearls, and in a moment even P.J. could see that any further discussion of the robbery was hopeless.

"Come on," she said, shaking loose of me. And with a final half-baffled, half-disgusted glance at Annalise, she headed out the door.

"I can't believe it," she said, shaking her head as I caught up with her on the sidewalk outside. "She recognized this necklace, and yet she said she'd never seen it before."

"Maybe she was scared," I suggested, searching for an explanation. "After all, Mr. Findletter told her not to talk about the robbery, and he's her boss. She might have been afraid—"

"Of what?" P.J. interrupted. "She says she's got the money to go back to college. She could quit tomorrow, so why wouldn't she want to talk about—"

Suddenly, she stopped. She stared at the flyer she held in her hand as if she were seeing it for the very first time.

"Wait a second," she said slowly, a peculiar expression coming over her face.

"What?" I leaned over to look at the flyer, too, but I didn't see anything I hadn't seen before. Just the picture, the description, the substantial reward stuff. What was it that P.J. had said? Substantial, that means a lot. Enough to buy all the furniture and file cabinets we want. Maybe even enough to finance our college educations.

"Oh, no," I murmured, an awful suspicion creeping into my mind. "P.J., you don't think she could have gotten the money for college by . . ." But one look at P.J. Clover's face told me that was *exactly* what she was thinking.

"But how about all that stuff about the robbery? The redheaded thief, the coughing fit . . . You don't seriously think the police were right, do you? You don't think she could have made all that up?"

I expected her to agree. It was impossible, after all. Ridiculous.

But she didn't.

Instead, she looked at the flyer again. "Well, there's one way to find out," she said, pointing to the phone number at the bottom of the page. "Come on!" She grabbed me by the arm and headed for the Mill Creek Market. "This case may be over, Stacy," she said, making a beeline for the bike rack. "Mr. Findletter may be O.O.B. by this afternoon!"

80

9

A Warning

By the time I figured out that O.O.B. meant out-of-business, P.J. had pulled the bike from the rack and swung her leg over the seat. "The clubhouse," she directed, motioning for me to hop on behind. "We'll call from there."

I hung on tight as she turned the bike into the street, narrowly missing a man in a dark suit and dark glasses who was about to get into his car. He'd taken our flyers from his windshield and was studying them, frowning.

Had he seen the redheaded thief?

The question flashed through my mind before I remembered. Maybe there hadn't been any thief. Maybe there hadn't been any robbery. Except the one carried out by Annalise Brown!

I didn't want to believe it.

Even if it meant that the case was solved, even if it meant that we'd found the necklace, that P.J.'s T-shirt collection was safe, and that Mr. Findletter's shady operations would be exposed, I *still* didn't want to be-

lieve it. Because it would mean that Annalise Brown had lied. It would mean that she'd made up that whole fantastic story and told it to the police, and to us, and to everyone else in Mill Creek. It was chilling just to think of. And if it were true, how would anyone be able to trust her again?

I don't think P.J. wanted to believe it either, but unlike me, P.J. Clover *always* faces facts, no matter how unpleasant they may be. She was facing them— the facts, I mean—right now. "It's easy to see how it could have happened," she said over her shoulder, as she swung the bike around the corner from Miller onto Sycamore and headed for our own block. "Those flyers were probably sent out to jewelry stores. Annalise probably saw one, filed it away somewhere, and when the necklace came in, the temptation was just too great. She took it when Mr. Findletter wasn't looking and—"

"But P.J.," I interrupted. Lying was bad enough, but stealing was worse. "You don't really think Annalise Brown is a thief."

"Well, she's got the money," P.J. said bluntly, her straggly blond hair blowing in my face as her words traveled back to my ears. "It has to have come from somewhere. And you saw how she acted when I showed her the flyer. And besides"—she made a sharp turn into our own block—"it wouldn't have been stealing. It would have been returning. Returning the necklace to its rightful owner!"

She was right, of course. But somehow it didn't make me feel any better. "Then why lie?" I said. "Why not just say she recognized the necklace and that it was stolen and . . ." But even as I spoke, I suddenly saw the

83

way it must have been. Because if Annalise had recognized the necklace, then she must have realized what Mr. Findletter, who'd been buying jewelry regularly from the same man, was up to. And if she realized what he was up to, then . . .

"P.J.!" I exclaimed, as we skidded to a halt in the Clovers' driveway. "I'll bet I know why she made up that story. I'll bet I know why she acted like she did. She was afraid!" I slid quickly off the bike. "Afraid of what Mr. Findletter might do if he knew that she knew."

"Exactly!" P.J. agreed grimly, dropping the bike on the drive and heading across the backyard. "This case may be bigger than we thought, Stacy. Mr. Findletter may have a lot more to hide than we imagined." She disappeared into the house and reappeared a moment later with the phone—one of those new cordless ones—in her hand.

"And people with a lot to hide," she said, ducking into the clubhouse with me at her heels, "are dangerous!"

I gulped. I hadn't been thinking about danger—not danger for us, anyway—but now that I did, I didn't like it.

"P.J., wait," I said as she glanced at the bottom of the flyer, which she'd pulled from her bookbag, and began to punch in the number. "Maybe we should think about this. I mean, what if we find out that Annalise did return the necklace and that Mr. Findletter did buy it knowing it was stolen. The police aren't going to arrest him. At least not right away. They'll just question him, and when he finds out that we were the ones who . . ."

But I was wasting my breath. Because P.J. was already talking to someone on the other end of the line.

"That's right," I heard her say as I stopped speaking and tuned back in. "The necklace that was stolen. The one that you— No, no, we don't have it, but . . ."

She shot a quick glance at me.

And I let out my breath, which I hadn't known I'd been holding. So! The necklace had *not* been returned. Annalise Brown had not told a lie. The case was not almost solved.

I saw P.J.'s hand go up to finger the lettering on the new orange T-shirt she was wearing. *Never Underestimate the Power of a Woman.* Butch wouldn't want that one, of course, but still . . .

"P.J., maybe . . ." I began. But before I could think of anything comforting to say, the expression on P.J.'s face changed.

"A joke?" she said, frowning. "No, this isn't a joke. We didn't call before."

She was stopped by a torrent of words coming over the line. I caught snatches—"children . . . shouldn't be allowed . . . toying with emotions . . . parents not doing their job . . ."

As the voice went on, P.J. looked more and more angry. Her cheeks turned red beneath her freckles. "But I tell you," she broke in, as soon as she got a chance, "it wasn't *us*! We may be kids, but we don't go around . . . Yes, yes, of course we'll let you know if—"

There was a loud click and then a humming sound as the line went dead. I heard it because P.J. was holding the phone away from her ear.

"The nerve!" she exclaimed, staring at the receiver as if she could hardly believe what had come out of it.

"Accusing *us* of playing jokes. Saying we'd called before. Saying we'd used some kind of crazy French accent."

"An accent?" Something suddenly clicked in my mind. "Wait a second, P.J. Didn't Annalise say that the thief had an accent?" As I spoke, I reached into the back pocket of my blue jeans and pulled out my notebook. I flipped through the pages. Yes, there it was. In black and white, after the red hair and sunglasses stuff. *Spoke with an accent. Probably French.*

P.J. grabbed the book from my hand. "You're right," she murmured, staring at the words. "But . . . but how . . . I mean, why? It doesn't make sense. Why would the thief call to ask if the necklace had been returned? If she . . . or he"—she must have suddenly remembered her theory about the thief being a man in disguise!— "has got it, then why . . . ?"

"I don't know," I admitted, feeling every bit as confused as P.J. "But at least it shows that it *wasn't* Annalise!"

"Maybe," P.J. said, frowning. "Or maybe . . ."

"No," I said, before she could begin wondering if Annalise was taking French in college, before she could start accusing her of putting on a phony French accent. "It wouldn't make any more sense for her to call than for the thief to call. I mean, if she took the necklace, she would have returned it to collect the reward. Obviously she hasn't, so why would she—"

"Then what's the explanation?" P.J. interrupted, slamming my notebook down on the table and running her fingers through her hair. "Where did she get the money for college?" she said, starting to pace back and forth in the crowded clubhouse. "If she didn't return the necklace, then how . . . ?"

"But P.J., she could have gotten it some other way," I said. "Maybe she had a rich uncle who died. Maybe she won the lottery."

"Then why didn't she tell us about it? If anything like that had happened, she wouldn't have kept it a secret. And why did she act so upset when I showed her the flyer? Why did she practically throw us out of the store? Think of it, Stacy." She stopped her pacing to stare at the flyer she still held in her hand. "She recognized this necklace, but she wouldn't admit it. She's got the money for college, but she wouldn't say how she got it. She was willing to talk to us yesterday, but not today. It doesn't add up. It doesn't make sense. Unless . . ." She paused and her eyes narrowed as if she were trying to pin down some thought that was flitting across the edges of her brain.

"What?" I said. "Unless what?"

"Unless," she repeated slowly—and now her nose gave an excited twitch—"she was *paid* to keep quiet!"

"Paid? You mean a bribe? But P.J.," I began, "Annalise would never . . ." Then I stopped. Because I suddenly realized that I no longer had any idea what Annalise Brown would or wouldn't do! Maybe she thought that going to college was such a good thing that doing something bad to get there was all right. Maybe Mr. Findletter had offered her the money, and she thought it would be impolite to refuse.

Then I thought of something. "P.J., wait," I said. "We're forgetting one thing. Annalise told us that Mr. Findletter's been worried about money. Well, college

87

costs a lot. If he's been having financial problems, then how could he come up with so much money? And anyway, how could it be worth it just to cover up one little crooked deal?"

"Little!" P.J. exclaimed. *Her* mind had obviously been racing ahead while mine had been plodding along trying to sort things out. "Listen, Stacy," she said now, "if keeping Annalise quiet is worth *that* much, then what we're seeing must be just the tip of the iceberg! This *little* robbery must threaten to expose something much bigger—some *enormous* operation. And if that's the case"—she paused, the expression on her face suddenly serious—"then Mr. Findletter wouldn't have to come up with the money all by himself."

"You mean . . . ?"

P.J. nodded as a picture of Mr. Findletter—mild-mannered Mr. Findletter—surrounded by a group of shadowy men in dark suits and dark glasses—organized crime!—popped into my mind. But that was crazy. I was letting my imagination run away with me. This was real life, not a TV show. "Nothing like that could happen in Mill Creek," I said.

But P.J. didn't agree. "Why not?" she countered. "It would explain where Mr. Findletter got the money. It would even explain how he got involved in the first place. He may not be a criminal himself, but if criminals approached him . . ."

Her voice trailed off, and I had to admit—much as I hated to think of it—that what she said *could* be true. It would certainly make sense, considering what we knew of Mr. Findletter. Because if he were involved with the Mob, then he might not be a crook at all. He might be just as much a victim as Annalise!

"If only we had proof," P.J. said, starting to pace back and forth again. "Some kind of evidence. Something that would show—" But before she could finish her sentence, she was interrupted by a sudden pounding on the clubhouse door.

I sprang for the peephole, half expecting to see a man in a dark suit and dark glasses, but before I could reach it, the door was shoved open and a boy, a boy with curly dark hair and freckles—Butch Bigelow!—pushed his way in.

He had his camera still slung around his neck, his aunt's book sticking out of one pocket, and a fistful of photographs in his hand.

"I've got it!" he announced triumphantly, waving the photos in P.J.'s face. "You thought I was nuts, but I was right! And now I've got proof. Proof that Mr. Findletter—"

P.J. snatched the photos from his hand. "What are you talking about?" she demanded. "What do you mean by pushing your way in here?" Then suddenly she stopped. She stared at the photos she held in her hand. I leaned over to look, and as I did, a chill traveled down my spine. There were five of them, all pretty much the same, all of Mr. Findletter standing outside Dilly's Ice Cream Parlor talking to a man in a dark suit and dark glasses—and I knew him! Or, at least, I'd seen him. I wasn't sure where, but— Then all at once I realized who it was. It was the man that P.J. had almost run over as we left the Mill Creek Market. The man who'd been reading our flyers!

P.J. recognized him, too. I could tell by the way she drew in her breath. But before she could say anything, Butch reached into his pocket and pulled out a small, rectangular-shaped object. A miniature tape recorder!

"Listen to this!" he said, sounding more excited now than triumphant. He set the recorder down on the table and switched it on. Background noises—dishes clattering, someone saying something about hot fudge—emerged from the tape. Then a voice that I recognized immediately as Mr. Findletter's began to speak.

"So this is it," he said. "The big payoff!"

P.J.'s eyes opened wide. "Stacy, did you hear that?" she said. "That means we were—"

"Right," a deeper sounding voice replied, as if it were completing P.J.'s sentence. "You're sure he'll have the stuff with him?"

"Oh, he'll have it, all right," Mr. Findletter said. "He assured me he'd be at my house at five this afternoon with—"

"Good," the other voice broke in. "Then I'll be there, too. It's 65 Sunnyside, right? The yellow house with the . . ." But the rest of his sentence was drowned out by a loud crash.

"Dishes," Butch explained quickly, switching the tape recorder off. "I thought he'd spotted me, so I knocked over a tray."

But P.J. wasn't interested in broken dishes. She grabbed the tape recorder from the table, holding it up as if it were a nugget of pure gold. "Stacy, this is it!" she said, as if Butch weren't even there. "*Exactly* what we've been looking for. *Exactly* what we need."

"You mean exactly what *I* need," Butch said, snatching the tape recorder and photos back. "This stuff proves that I was right. Mr. Findletter's a drug dealer, just like I said he was, just like that guy in my aunt's book. And now I'm going to take all this to the police and—"

But before Butch could go anywhere, and before either P.J. or I could say a word about what Mr. Findletter was *really* up to, the clubhouse door burst open again and a woman in a green dress—P.J.'s mother—followed by a man in a blue uniform—the police!—stepped inside. The officer had a bunch of papers in his hand. P.J.'s mother had an angry—or maybe it was just an exasperated—look on her face.

"P.J. Clover," she said. "And you, too, Stacy Jones. What have you gotten yourselves into *this* time?"

Another person—a lesser person—would have hesitated at a remark like that, but *not* P.J.! Hardly missing a beat, hardly seeming to think about what a police officer was doing in our clubhouse, she grabbed the photos and tape recorder from Butch's hand. "Crime!" she replied, as he opened his mouth to protest. "*Real* crime. And now we've got proof. Proof that Mr. Findletter—"

"Now wait a second," the police officer said. "I don't know what you kids are up to, but if it has anything to do with the robbery at Findletter's Jewelry Store—"

"You're to stay out of it!" Mrs. Clover interrupted. "Honestly, P.J., this is going too far. Finding things for people in the neighborhood is one thing, but going after a real thief . . . ? Well, I'm just glad the police found these flyers you made"—she gestured to the papers in the police officer's hand—"before it was too late!"

"Too late?" P.J. exclaimed. "But that's *exactly* what it's going to be if we don't do something soon! Look at

91

these," she said, thrusting the photos at the police officer. "And there's a tape recording, too. Of Mr. Findletter and that man setting up a meeting. They're planning to—"

"*I'm* the one who made it," Butch interrupted, pushing himself forward. "Inside Dilly's Ice Cream Parlor."

The police officer held up his hand. "All right, all right," he said, tucking the photos—which he'd hardly looked at—into his pocket. "I'll take these down to the station with me. We'll do whatever has to be done, but meanwhile, I want you kids to stay out of it."

"Stay out?" P.J. said. "But—"

"No buts," the officer interrupted. "I'm not sure what all this is about myself, but the chief says he doesn't want you mixed up in it. Too dangerous, he says, and that's good enough for me."

"And for me," P.J.'s mother put in. "I want you girls—and you, too, Butch—to promise you'll work on something sensible. Like this." She took one of the flyers from the police officer's hand. "Baby Cuddles. Now think of how happy you'd be making that little girl if you found her. And if all three of you worked together, you'd do it in no time."

"Together," Butch snorted. "Me look for a stupid old doll? I'd rather—"

"Now wait a second," I broke in angrily. "It was you who—"

But P.J. didn't give me a chance to finish. "Wait a minute," she said, a peculiar look on her face. "Maybe they're right. Maybe we shouldn't get involved in anything dangerous. Maybe we should stick to helping poor little Tina."

92

Poor little Tina? I could hardly believe my ears. "You mean you think we *should* stay out of it?" I said.

"A wise decision," the police officer put in.

Mrs. Clover looked relieved.

Butch looked confused. "Wait a second!" he exclaimed, as the officer and P.J.'s mother turned to go. "You can't just—" But P.J. stopped him with a fierce scowl and a sharp elbow to the ribs. He didn't recover until the door had swung shut behind Mrs. Clover and the police officer. Then he turned on P.J. angrily. "What do you think you're doing?" he demanded. "How could you let him take all that evidence? He'll probably say he collected it himself and we—I mean, I—won't get any credit."

"Shhh," P.J. hissed, putting her eye to the peephole and holding up her hand for silence. "Okay," she whispered after a moment. "They're gone. Quick, Stacy, the map."

I didn't know what was going on and I didn't stop to ask. I just grabbed the map of Mill Creek from the bookshelf and spread it out on the table.

"Sunnyside," P.J. murmured, paying no attention to Butch's continued sputtering. She ran her finger over the streets. "Sixty-five, right?" She glanced at the clock on the wall. "It's four thirty now, and it'll take us fifteen minutes to get there."

"You mean . . ." Butch stopped sputtering. "But I thought you said they were right. I thought you promised to stay out of it."

"I said *maybe* they were right. And I didn't promise anything. Don't you see?" she said. "We *can't* stay out of it now. Not now when we know what they're up to!"

94

Butch looked blank. And for a moment, I didn't see what she was getting at either. Then it hit me. It was her old *Trust no one ... suspect everyone* rule. "But P.J., you can't be serious," I said. "You can't really think that the police would ..."

"Why not?" she countered. "It's happened before. Maybe not here in Mill Creek, but in other places."

"You mean ...?" Light suddenly dawned on Butch Bigelow's face. "You're right!" he exclaimed. "It happens all the time in my aunt's books. There's something crooked going on and the police know all about it, but they keep quiet because the criminal makes it worth their while. That's *got* to be it," he said excitedly. "Why else would they try to scare us off? Why else would they want to pin the whole thing on Annalise?"

"Exactly!" P.J. agreed (not seeming to notice who she was agreeing with!). She grabbed the tape recorder from the table and slipped it into her pocket. "We'll take this," she said, heading for the door. "We'll record everything that goes on at this meeting of theirs and then ..." She paused. "We'll turn it all over ... to the reporters at the *Morning Gazette!*"

So *that* was her plan! The power of the press.

"But P.J.," I said. "Don't you think we should ...?" I wasn't sure what I was going to say, because I wasn't sure what I thought we should do. But it didn't matter anyway, because P.J. was already halfway across the yard with Butch hot on her heels. By the time I got out of the clubhouse, she was grabbing her bike from where she'd dropped it on the drive. And by the time I reached the drive, she was swinging her leg over the seat.

"Hey!" I yelled. "Wait for me!" But it was too late.
Butch—Butch Bigelow!—had hopped on behind. And
P.J. didn't seem to care! Her straggly blond hair was
blowing in his face, and he was hanging on tight as she
swung out into the street.

"Get your bike," she shouted, not even bothering to
turn around to see me standing all by myself on the
drive. "Sixty-five Sunnyside. We'll meet you there!"

10

The Perfect Disguise

I could hardly believe it was happening.

P.J. and Butch. Butch and P.J. Together! I'd been saying for years they should bury the hatchet, but I never expected it to happen like this. I never expected that *I'd* be the one left behind!

How could P.J. do it? How could she let Butch, who had his greedy little eyes on her T-shirts, hop on behind instead of me? How could she tell me to get my bike when she knew it was locked away, when she knew *why* it was locked away!

A vision of my ten-speed, bent like a pretzel, flashed through my mind. Was there any hope of saving it now? Was there any hope that P.J. would care about finding Tina's doll once she had her picture in all the papers, her name in the news? Once she exposed the criminals, found the necklace, and . . . But no. That was wrong. P.J. *wasn't* going to find the necklace. P.J. wasn't even on the trail of the necklace anymore! She was after Mr. Findletter and the man with dark glasses and . . . Suddenly an awful thought struck me. Butch—sneaky old, crafty old Butch Bigelow—could still win the bet!

P.J. wouldn't be thinking of that, of course—that was the sort of thing *I* thought of for her. Butch might not be thinking of it, either. Not now. But when tomorrow came . . . I could practically hear him. "It's not that I *want* to do it," he'd say, like an echo of the terrible Toomeys, "but I *have* to. A bet's a bet, after all. It's the principle of the thing." And that would be the end. The end of Wonder Woman, Mickey Mouse, Carlsbad Caverns, the works!

I couldn't let it happen. Even if P.J. didn't care about my bike, even if she was ready to ride off with Butch, I *still* couldn't let it happen. We'd been friends too long, we'd been through too much. Yet what could I do? Together we hadn't come close to finding the necklace. Was there any chance that I could find it alone?

I pulled my notebook from my pocket and began to flip through the pages. It was what P.J. had said we should do in the first place—"go through your notes, sift them for evidence, search them for clues." She'd never gotten around to it, of course. She'd been too carried away with her theories about Mr. Findletter, with her dreams of solving bigger and bigger crimes. But it was a good idea, and right now it was the only one I could think of.

Quickly I scanned through Annalise's words. At least now we knew they were true. There really had been a robbery, there really had been a thief. She'd tried on the necklace and started to cough, and when Annalise ran into the back room to get a glass of water, she'd disappeared. But where had she gone? Where was there to go? Just the street out front, the pet shop next door, the passageway in between where Tina Toomey's doll carriage had been—

Then suddenly I stopped. The hairs on the back of my neck seemed to stand on end. I felt as if a window were opening in my mind as, all at once, the scene in the Toomeys' kitchen came back to me. Tina's accusation ("She's the one who took my Baby Cuddles!"), her father's denial ("It's just an idea she's gotten into her head"), P.J.'s dismissal ("You just told us you didn't see anyone, so how do you know—"). But suppose Tina had been right. Suppose we had been wrong.

I narrowed my eyes and tried to picture the scene. The redheaded thief coming out of the jewelry store, nervous, afraid, looking for a place to hide. She'd know she couldn't get away without being noticed, not dressed the way she was. So she'd duck into the passageway. She'd see the carriage with Baby Cuddles sleeping peacefully inside. And Mrs. Toomey's scarf. Suddenly I realized how important that was! Her eyes would light up. She'd—

But just then, just as I was about to picture what the thief would do next, a shout made me turn around to see Tina Toomey racing down the block. She was yelling and waving wildly in my direction with one hand and dragging an embarrassed-looking boy behind her with the other.

"Where is she?" she cried, skidding to a halt in the Clovers' drive, her face red, her chest heaving. "The eye. The *real* eye. I've got to find her."

The boy wrenched himself out of her grasp. "Are you crazy?" he said, rubbing his arm where she'd been gripping it. "I try to help and you . . ." He looked ready to bolt, but Tina wasn't about to let him. She grabbed him by the arm before he could get away.

"He knows!" she exclaimed, forgetting about P.J. (the real eye!) and turning to me. "You wouldn't believe me. No one would believe me. But he saw! He found one of the flyers Mommy and Daddy made, and he came to tell me. My baby, my poor—"

"She means her doll," the boy interrupted, wrenching himself free again.

"Her doll?" I said. My heart skipped a beat.

The boy went on talking. "I just figured I'd help, but I didn't know it would be like this. Her dragging me over here, yelling like crazy so the whole neighborhood could hear. I think I know some guys who live on this block," he added nervously. "I wouldn't want them to . . ."

But I didn't care about his friends. I didn't care what they might think. "What did you see?" I demanded, grabbing the boy by the shoulders and giving him a shake. "Who did you see? Who took her?"

The boy opened his mouth to reply, but Tina didn't give him a chance. "*She* took her!" she exclaimed. "Just like I said she did. Just like *you* wouldn't believe she did! She reached into the carriage and—"

"But I didn't know she was a thief," the boy protested, struggling out of my grip. "If I'd known, I would have stopped her. All I saw was this redheaded woman."

"She took Mommy's scarf, too," Tina said. "And she wrapped it around her head."

"You couldn't see her hair then," the boy put in. "You couldn't tell it was a doll she was holding, either, because she carried it like a baby, a real baby," he said.

And suddenly the whole thing was perfectly clear! Tina had been right. The crimes we were trying to solve *were* connected. But we hadn't been able to see it. We'd been blind to the truth because we couldn't imagine Baby Cuddles being valuable to anyone but Tina. But she was. Lying there in her carriage outside Findletter's Jewelry Store, she was exactly what the thief had needed—a disguise, a perfect disguise!

It couldn't have been planned, of course. It must have been done on the spur of the moment, like an actress improvising a part in a play. But once the thief had thought of it, it would have been easy. All she had to do was grab the scarf, wrap it around her head, pick up Baby Cuddles, and walk away. No one would suspect that she'd just stolen a valuable antique necklace, because she wouldn't look like a thief. She would look like an ordinary Mill Creek mother out taking her baby for a walk!

It was incredible. And I only wished that P.J. were here to hear it. To learn that, in one fell swoop, her T-shirts had been saved, my bike had been rescued, and . . . But wait! That was wrong, I suddenly realized. Nothing had been saved! Nothing had been solved. Tina still didn't have her doll, P.J. still didn't have the necklace. We didn't know who the redheaded robber was or where she'd gone or . . .

Desperately, I grabbed the boy by the shoulders again. "Where did she go?" I cried, shaking him as if words would fall out of his mouth like pennies from a bank. "Did she catch a bus? Get into a car?" I knew a license number was too much to hope for, but if he could describe what it looked like, maybe the police could find it.

But Tina wasn't about to waste any more time.

"There wasn't any car," she declared. "There was a house."

"A house?" I echoed. "You mean here? In Mill Creek?"

"Well, of course," Tina said, as if I were some kind of dummy. "Where else would it be? She walked there and he followed. He had his dog with him and—"

"It's a big dog," the boy said. "I had him on his leash and when that woman took the baby—I mean, the doll—and started down the street, my dog decided to go in the same direction. I didn't mean to follow her, but that's how it turned out. We trailed her all the way to this house and—"

"That's where she is now!" Tina broke in. "My baby, my poor baby." Her voice suddenly trembled, her eyes filled with tears. "She's cold and she's hungry and . . . and we've got to rescue her before it's too late!"

The boy looked disgusted. "It's only a doll," he began. "Dolls don't—"

I didn't give him a chance to finish. "The address," I said quickly, feeling as if the whole thing might vanish if I didn't act fast. "Just give us the address."

The boy shook his head. "Can't," he replied. "I didn't see any street signs or numbers."

Tina rumbled ominously.

"But I *think* I know where it is," he added quickly. "I *think* I can find it again."

"You'd better," Tina warned, wiping her nose on the back of her sleeve. "You'd better or my brothers . . ."

But I didn't need the threat of the Toomey twins to make me move. "Come on," I said, sounding more like P.J. Clover than myself. "We're going to find your baby. We're going to find that necklace. We're going to find them both or . . ." I hesitated. (I wasn't used to doing things like this without P.J., after all!) But then I took a deep breath. "We're going to find them both," I said, "or . . . my name's not Stacy Jones, private eye!"

I don't know how we got to the center of town. We must have run. But I can't remember. My mind was racing too fast to notice what my feet were doing.

"I think I can find it from here," the boy said as we passed the Mill Creek Market. "I think I'll recognize the block she turned on."

I wished that he sounded a bit more certain. I wished that I *felt* a bit more certain. Because now that we were on our way, I suddenly realized that I didn't know what we would do when we got there. We couldn't just knock on the door. The house might be full of thieves. And even though *I* might be willing to take the risk—I was a private eye, after all—I couldn't put a couple of kids in danger. Not even P.J. Clover would do that!

Maybe we should call the police, I thought nervously as the boy turned a corner and led us away from the center of town.

"I'm pretty sure it's this way," he murmured. "I think that's the fire hydrant my dog stopped at. I think we turned left."

103

They'd have to come, wouldn't they? Even though they *had* warned us to stay out of the case. Even though they *might* be involved in whatever Mr. Findletter was up to. But I didn't want to think about that. I didn't want to think about the Mill Creek police being involved in anything crooked!

"Where is this place?" Tina said, breaking into my thoughts as the boy hesitated before leading us around another corner. "I thought you said you could find it. I thought you knew where it was."

"I do," he protested. "Sort of. It's just that I didn't notice everything and . . . Wait a second!" he exclaimed. He signaled for us to stop. We were at the end of a long block of comfortable looking houses. "I think that's it! The yellow house. The one with the blue car parked in the drive, halfway down the block. I'm not absolutely sure, but I think that's where she went. I think . . ."

But even as he spoke, the side door of the house was flung open and a young woman stepped out. She had dark hair, not red. She was wearing blue jeans, a down jacket, a canvas hat, and carrying a sleeping bag under one arm. I caught my breath. I was sure that I'd seen her before. I didn't know where, I didn't know when, but . . . She glanced nervously up and down the block as if she were afraid someone might be watching. Then she pulled down the brim of her hat and headed straight for the car parked in the drive.

"I'm getting out of here," I heard the boy, who was standing beside me, say. "I don't know if that's her, I don't know if that's the house. And I'm not going to stick around to find out!"

104

He was gone before I could stop him. And I didn't even know his name. If this wasn't the house, if this wasn't the thief, we might never be able to find him again!

The girl, meanwhile, had tossed her sleeping bag into the car and slipped into the driver's seat.

I knew I should stop her.

Even though this might be the wrong house, even though she didn't have red hair, even though she was probably just some innocent high school girl I'd seen around town, I knew I shouldn't let her get away. I should run down the block yelling and shouting. I should question her. I should . . . But my voice seemed to have disappeared. My legs wouldn't move.

I heard the car engine start. And suddenly Tina, who I'd almost forgotten about, let out a shout. "Stop!" she yelled. She broke away from my side and raced down the block. "Wait! Where's my baby? You can't leave without . . ."

But the young woman didn't stop. She pulled the car out of the drive and swung it into the street, tires squealing.

And now I *had* to move. I raced after Tina. There was no telling what she might do—grab onto a fender, pull open the door. She'd already reached the edge of the drive. She was ready to dash into the street. But then suddenly, she stopped. Suddenly, she *was* stopped! Her head was jerked back, her legs were lifted off the ground as something—*someone*—hidden in the bushes that bordered the drive grabbed her and dragged her, kicking and screaming, into the shrubbery.

This time I didn't hesitate. My heart was pounding, my knees were trembling, but I plunged into the bushes after her. "Let go of her!" I shouted, not knowing who I was shouting at. "I'll call the police. I'll—"

A hand was clapped over my mouth. An arm was wrapped around my neck. "Where have you been?" someone hissed in my ear. "What took you so long? Why did you bring *her*?"

▌▌

Trapped!

I pulled the hand from my mouth and stared at P.J. Clover in astonishment. Beside her in the bushy undergrowth, I could see Tina being held firmly by Butch. She'd stopped struggling, but she looked as if she might bite off his fingers, maybe his whole hand, at any moment.

"You?" I said, feeling as if I'd stepped into some kind of time—or place—warp. "But how . . . where . . . I mean, what . . . what are *you* doing here?"

"Waiting for you," Butch replied impatiently. "We could have been in there ages ago."

"You mean . . . ?" I peered out of the bushes at the house. For the first time, I noticed the address on the mailbox—65 Sunnyside. "You mean this is Mr. Findletter's house?" I said.

"Well, of course," P.J. replied. "And we *couldn't* have been in there ages ago," she said turning to Butch. "We had to wait for his daughter to leave, and now that she has, it'll be easy. She didn't even lock the door and—"

"His daughter?" I interrupted. "You mean that's who—"

"Took my baby!" Tina exclaimed, breaking out of Butch's grip. "She's the one. He saw her. She took my Baby Cuddles!"

P.J. looked startled. "Mr. Findletter's daughter? Took your doll? But that's crazy," she said. "Why would she—"

Butch had had enough. "Who knows?" he interrupted. "Who cares? We've wasted enough time already. We've got to get into that house."

"You're right," P.J. said quickly, not about to let Butch take over! "I don't know what all this is about, but we don't have time to find out now. So just leave her"—she indicated Tina with a jerk of her thumb—"here and . . ."

But Tina wasn't about to be left anywhere. "I'm coming!" she declared. "My baby's in there. She's cold and she's hungry."

"Better take her," Butch warned. "No telling what she'll do if we leave her out here."

I could see that P.J. wasn't happy. Not about getting advice from Butch, nor about dragging a crazed four year old along with her. But what could she do? "All right," she agreed, scowling fiercely at Tina. "But you'd better behave yourself. Now come on," she said, starting to crawl out of the bushes. "There's no time to lose!"

"But P.J.," I began. My mind was turning in circles. Could Tina be right? I tried to remember what we knew

109

about Mr. Findletter's daughter. I still couldn't recall where I'd seen her before, but I did remember that she'd been giving Mr. Findletter a hard time, that she wanted to drop out of school and go to New York to become an actress. That would take money, of course. Lots of it. But would she actually steal from her own father? And what about Mr. Findletter himself? Could what *she* might have done be connected with what *he* might be doing? Or maybe the whole thing was a mistake! Maybe the boy had been wrong about the house. Maybe . . .

But there was no time for any more thought. P.J. and Butch were already out of the bushes and dashing across the drive with Tina, still muttering about Baby Cuddles, hot on their heels. I pulled myself together—what else could I do?—and ran after them, reaching the door just as P.J. pushed it open and stepped inside. I hesitated. But there was no turning back. Butch gave me a shove, and the door swung shut behind us. I was in it, and in it for good!

The house was quiet (as still as a tomb, I thought!), and for a moment none of us spoke. I knew it was wrong—definitely wrong—to enter someone's house when they weren't at home, and I could see that P.J. was having doubts, too. But she recovered herself quickly. "It's all right," she said, as if she were trying to convince herself just as much as me. "*He's* been breaking the law. We have to break the law to stop him!" She pulled Butch's tape recorder from her pocket. "Now, where's the best place to put this?" she said, before anyone could raise any objections.

"The living room," Butch replied quickly, as if he

110

bugged people's houses every day. "If they're having a meeting that's where they'll . . ."

P.J. was already halfway down the hallway before he could finish his sentence. "*Exactly* what we need!" I heard her exclaim as she ducked through a doorway at the end. I reached the living room just in time to see her pounce on a large leafy plant standing on the coffee table. She parted the leaves, nestled the tape recorder inside, and clicked on the switch.

Butch looked impressed—nervous, but impressed. "Perfect," he said. "They'll never find it in there. Now, if only it'll work," he added anxiously. "Sometimes the tape gets stuck."

"Stuck!" P.J. exclaimed. "But we can't risk . . . I mean, this is our only chance. How else are we going to get anyone to believe us? How else are we going to prove what Mr. Findletter's up to?" She looked desperately around the room. I could see her dreams of glory slipping away. Then, suddenly, her eyes fell on a narrow door in the far wall. "Wait a second!" she said. "That looks like a closet. We could hide in there. Then if the recorder doesn't work, at least we'll all be witnesses. We'll all have heard . . ."

But now *I* had heard enough. "Are you crazy, P.J.?" I said. "We can't stay here. We shouldn't be here in the first place. If Mr. Findletter ever found us . . ."

But just then, before I could begin to describe what Mr. Findletter might do, an ominous sound came from the driveway. A car! I heard an engine roar and then fall silent, a door slam. Butch sprang to a window. "Oh, no!" he exclaimed. "It's—"

"The thief?" Tina cried. She'd been silent—wide-

111

eyed and silent—up until now but, at the sound of the car, the haunted look of a grief-stricken mother returned to her face. "The one who stole my baby? Is she back? Is she—"

P.J. clapped a hand over Tina's mouth. "Quick," she said, motioning to the narrow door at the end of the room. "In there!"

Butch leaped away from the window, pulled open the door, and we tumbled inside.

It was a closet! And a huge one. It must have been used for storage, because it smelled of mothballs and musty wool. There were coats on the rods and boxes on the floor. A small, dusty window let in a faint glow of light. Tina was still struggling as we quickly moved to the back of the closet and crammed ourselves in behind the coats. "Let me go," she demanded, her voice muffled by P.J.'s hand. "I want my baby. You can't . . ."

I could hear men's voices coming from the hallway. Desperately, I grabbed Tina by the straps of her overalls. "Listen to me," I hissed in her ear. "Your baby's not here. That boy made a mistake." I was convinced of it now. It would have been crazy, after all, for Mr. Findletter's daughter to take the necklace and even crazier for any other thief to come here. "But wherever she is," I went on, "you'll never see her again if you don't keep quiet. You'll never see anything again because you'll be . . ."

But before I could say "dead," Tina stopped struggling. The voices were in the living room now, and I guess that even *she* must have recognized the danger we were in! She shrank back meekly against a box of old clothes. In the dim light, I could see the look of relief on P.J. Clover's face.

My heart was pounding. What had we gotten ourselves into? All I'd wanted was to save P.J.'s T-shirts, all I'd wanted was to rescue my bike, and now . . .

In the living room a deep voice—the same deep voice that we'd heard on Butch's tape—spoke out. "He'll be here any minute," he said. "Have you got your microphone ready?"

Mr. Findletter must have nodded.

"Good," the man said. "Remember, it's important that we get as much on tape as possible."

On tape? I shot a quick glance at P.J. In the dim light, I could see that she was frowning. Butch, half-hidden by an overcoat, was too. Why would Mr. Findletter want to record anything on tape? Tape was evidence—the kind of stuff P.J. was planning to take to the *Morning Gazette*. Surely if Mr. Findletter was involved in anything crooked he wouldn't want a tape of it lying around.

"I don't know," he said now. "This makes me nervous. Suppose the microphone doesn't work. Suppose the tape gets stuck. Suppose—"

"Don't worry," the other man broke in. "I've been through this before. And anyway, if anything goes wrong, I'll be right in here."

His voice was close to the closet as he spoke, and suddenly an awful suspicion entered my mind. I glanced at P.J. Even in the dim light I could see that she'd turned pale beneath her freckles.

"The minute he's taken the money," the man was saying, "I'll send the signal and—"

113

He was interrupted by the sound of a car pulling into the drive. Again, I heard an engine stop, a door slam.

"All right. This is it!" the man outside the closet said. "Now don't be nervous. And remember, if you have any trouble, I'll be *right in here.*"

And with that, he pulled the closet door open and stepped inside!

I'd never felt so scared in all my life!

We were trapped. Trapped in a dark, musty closet with . . . But I had no idea who—or what—this man was! I shrank back against a box of old clothes. It was lucky the closet was so large. Otherwise the man surely would have seen us. Still, I wished I could disappear. I wished we could all disappear. I wished I'd never heard of Mr. Findletter. I wished P.J. had never dreamed of solving a real crime. I wished—

Then suddenly, my knee joint cracked. I froze. It sounded loud as a gunshot to me, but incredibly, the man didn't seem to notice. He was concentrating on a small metal box that he'd pulled from his jacket. With one swift motion, he extended a rod from the top (a walkie-talkie, I realized) and then held the box close to his lips. "Stand by," he whispered into it, his voice low and urgent. "He's approaching the house. It'll be all over soon."

All over soon? A chill traveled down my spine at the sound of those words. What would be over? Who was he talking to?

Once again, voices were coming from the living room. Mr. Findletter and another man were talking. They said something about diamonds. Something about pearls. The man in the closet was listening intently. He slipped his hand into his jacket. Did he have a holster hidden there? Could he be reaching for . . . ?

Suddenly I remembered all those old movies I'd seen on TV—movies I wasn't supposed to be watching—about gangsters muscling in on each other's territories, sending grizzly warnings (like severed ears and horses' heads), laying traps, bumping each other off. Could that be what was going on here?

I shrank back farther, digging my hand into the box of old clothes. And suddenly my fingers touched something—something firm, cool, yet strangely fleshy. The hair on the back of my neck rose. Skin! That's what it felt like. Skin that had . . . In a flash, everything I'd ever heard about bodies—*dead* bodies—raced through my mind. I jerked my hand from the box, not caring how much noise I made. Beside me, I heard Tina gasp.

Outside the closet, Mr. Findletter was saying, "All right, I'm going to give you the money."

Inside the closet, the man with the walkie-talkie was whispering, "This is it. Get ready."

And then, Tina screamed. Not just a little scream, but a huge, ear-piercing, hear-it-in-the-next-house, hear-it-on-the-next-block screech.

"My baby!"

She pounced on the box. She grabbed a tiny hand. She pulled a small, stiff body from the clothes. "My baby!" she cried, holding the body up as the closet door burst open and Mr. Findletter and a short, bald-headed man peered in. "My Baby Cuddles!"

12

The Final Operation

For a moment everything seemed to stop. It was as if we were frozen—suspended for an instant in time. Then suddenly, everything—everyone—sprang into action again.

The bald-headed man uttered an oath, backed away from the closet, and started to run.

"Stop him!" the man with the walkie-talkie shouted. He started to run himself, but before he had gone two feet, P.J. burst out of the closet, grabbed him by the back of his jacket, and hung on like a terrier as he stumbled and fell to the floor.

"Get the others," she shouted. "Don't let them get away!"

Butch, not to be outdone, charged after the bald-headed man.

I stumbled out of the closet, still reeling from the shock of touching that cold, hard flesh. Baby Cuddles! So the boy had been right! The thief *had* come

116

to this house. And that meant, that must mean . . .

But there was no time to think about the robbery now. Mr. Findletter was reaching for the walkie-talkie that had been knocked from the man's hands.

"Don't let him get it!" P.J. cried.

I flung myself on top of it. I didn't know who was on the other end. I didn't know what was going on. But in that split second, I knew that I couldn't let it fall into Mr. Findletter's hands. I rolled out of his reach, the walkie-talkie clutched to my chest. Out of the corner of my eye, I saw Butch bring the bald-headed man down with a flying tackle. And suddenly, the whole thing seemed like some sort of movie—some sort of crazy and *dangerous* movie. How would it end? How *could* it end? We couldn't fight off three grown men forever. It was just a matter of time before . . .

Then suddenly, I heard footsteps pounding down the hall. "Freeze!" a voice commanded as three uniformed officers appeared in the living room doorway. "Everybody freeze!"

The police!

A feeling of relief swept over me.

I recognized the officer who'd come to our clubhouse. I'd seen the other two officers around town, too. *They* wouldn't let anything happen to us. Now that they were here, we were . . . But then, I thought of something. Why were they here? We hadn't sent for them. How could they have known we were in trouble? How could they have known to come charging in at just this moment unless . . . I stared at the walkie-talkie still clutched in my hand, at the label taped neatly across the bottom. PROPERTY OF MILL CREEK POLICE DEPART-MENT, it read!

"I'll take that," the officer standing nearest to me said.

P.J. was on her feet in a flash. "Don't give it to her!" she cried. "It's evidence. They're in this together." She snatched the walkie-talkie from my hand and dived for Butch's tape recorder hidden in the plant. But the man she had tackled was too quick for her. He leaped to his feet. "Don't let him get away," he shouted to the officers who were struggling with Butch and the bald-headed man. Then he grabbed P.J. by the back of her shirt. "Hold it right there, young lady," he said angrily. "I want an explanation."

"And so do I!" Mr. Findletter said. "I told you girls to stay out of this. I told you this was no place for a couple of kids."

"I tried to stop them," the officer who'd come to our clubhouse put in. He'd managed to pull the man Butch had tackled up from the floor, separate him from Butch, and twist an arm behind his back. He held him tight while the other officer unfastened a pair of hand-cuffs from his belt.

"I want to talk to my lawyer," the man protested as the officer snapped the cuffs on his wrists. "I *demand* to talk to my lawyer!"

Now I was really confused. What was going on? It looked like the bald-headed man was being arrested. But how could that be? If this whole thing was a crimi-nal operation, if the police were involved, then . . .

"You've got nothing on me," the man said. "No proof. No evidence."

"No evidence?" Mr. Findletter echoed, forgetting about P.J. and me and turning on the handcuffed man. "Why, I've been keeping records on you for months. I told the police the very first day you came into my store peddling your stolen goods. The only reason they didn't arrest you right then and there is that the F.B.I.—"

"The F.B.I.!" Butch exclaimed. "You mean . . . ?"

"That's right." The man who'd been hiding in the closet with us let go of P.J.'s shirt, reached into his pocket, and pulled out a small leather case. "Special Agent Burns, Federal Bureau of Investigation," he said, flipping open the case—which had an identity card in it—and holding it out for us to see.

P.J. stared at the card.

Butch looked like he was about to fall through the floor. "*You* attacked an officer of the F.B.I.," he said, regarding P.J. with awe.

"And *you* attacked someone who's been wanted in five states," the F.B.I. agent said. "Luckily, this fellow's not dangerous," he added quickly as Butch's chest began to swell with pride. "But we've been after him for a long time. We might never have had enough evidence to build a case against him if Mr. Findletter here hadn't been willing to help."

"You mean, *you* were working with *them*?" P.J. said, turning to Mr. Findletter in astonishment. "But we thought . . . that is, it seemed like . . . I mean, from the way you acted . . ." Her voice trailed off, her face turned red.

The expression on Mr. Findletter's face softened slightly. "Well, I suppose it did look suspicious," he

119

said. "But we couldn't have you girls snooping around, trying to investigate that ridiculous robbery just when we were getting ready to—"

P.J. didn't give him a chance to finish. "The robbery!" she exclaimed, seizing on the word as if it were a crust of bread thrown to a starving man. "Stacy, we forgot about the robbery!"

"Oh, no, we didn't," I began. "We . . ."

But P.J. had already forgotten about me. She turned on the bald-headed man accusingly. I could see that she was desperate. Not to save her T-shirts (she probably wasn't even thinking about them), but to save face in front of Mr. Findletter, and Butch, and the man from the F.B.I.! "You did it, didn't you?" she said, before I could stop her. "You sold that necklace to Mr. Findletter, and then you were so greedy that you stole it back again. You dressed up as a woman and—"

"Now wait a second," the man interrupted. "I'm no weirdo!"

"That's right," Mr. Findletter agreed. "Just look at him. He could never pass for a woman. And besides, it wouldn't have been worth the risk. I'm afraid that whatever happened to that necklace is still a mystery. I have no idea who—"

"Oh, yes, you do!" a voice exclaimed.

It was Tina! She emerged from the closet, her Baby Cuddles in one arm, a bunch of clothes in the other. "You lie," she declared, pointing a pudgy little finger at Mr. Findletter. "That robber came right into this house. She stuffed my Baby Cuddles into a box in that closet, and then she piled her yucky old clothes on top of her. Look!" She dumped the armload of clothes at Mr. Findletter's feet.

120

I caught my breath as a pair of rhinestone-studded sunglasses and a bright red wig rolled onto the floor along with a dark-colored dress and long white gloves.

P.J.'s eyes opened wide. "Then it really was . . ." She exchanged a quick glance with me. She didn't have all the pieces, of course. She didn't know all that I knew. But I could see that she was rapidly completing the picture. She stared at Mr. Findletter, at the shocked expression that had come over his face as he stooped to pick up the wig. "Your daughter," she said, lowering her voice to almost a whisper. "Your very own daughter."

"No!" Mr. Findletter exclaimed. "It couldn't be. These are her costumes. She keeps them in a box in that closet. But someone else must have used them. She's an impulsive girl, she sometimes does things without thinking, but she would never . . ."

But before he could say "steal," the living room door burst open and a plump, blond-haired girl rushed in. "Oh, Mr. Findletter," she cried, hardly seeming to notice the police—to say nothing of the rest of us. "She didn't mean to do it. It was all a mistake. She was just trying to show you how well she could act. And when you weren't there, she got carried away and she took the necklace. She didn't know that you were dealing in stolen goods, and now . . . now she's gone, run away and . . ." She stopped, stared at the police as if she were seeing them for the very first time, and clapped her hand over her mouth. "Oh, no," she said. "Now I've done it. Finny will never forgive me!"

Finny? Suddenly I remembered the teenager I'd collided with outside the girls' lavatory. So *that* was

121

Mr. Findletter's daughter! That was where I'd seen her before. No wonder she'd looked so shocked when she saw the flyer that dropped from my hand. That flyer had told her that the necklace she'd stolen from her father's store was already stolen property!

Mr. Findletter's face had turned white. "Run away," he murmured. "I was afraid this would happen. I was afraid she would . . ." He grabbed the blond-haired girl by the shoulders. "Where did she go?" he demanded. "You're her best friend. She must have told you."

But the girl shook her head. "I don't know where she went. All she told me was that she was hiding the necklace and—"

"Hiding the necklace!" I could see from the look on P.J.'s face that she suddenly had remembered what would happen if she didn't get it back. "Where did she hide it?" she said urgently. "Is it here in this house? Is it—"

But Mr. Findletter cut her off. "What does it matter?" he said impatiently. "The necklace isn't important. It's my daughter, my poor Finella."

The blond-haired girl put her hand on his arm. "Don't worry, Mr. Findletter," she said quickly. "I'm sure she's coming back. She said she was hiding the necklace in a safe place and going away to think. I couldn't stop her—I tried—but at least I got her to promise that no matter what, she'd call you tomorrow."

"Tomorrow!" P.J. exclaimed, before Mr. Findletter could even open his mouth. "What time tomorrow?"

"Two o'clock," the girl replied promptly. "She promised—absolutely, cross her heart and hope to die—that she'd call home tomorrow at two o'clock sharp!"

122

I'd never seen P.J. Clover so miserable.

We searched, of course. The house, the yard, the garage, even the jewelry store (where we learned that Annalise had gotten the money for college from a scholarship, which she wasn't supposed to discuss before it was announced, *not* from Mr. Findletter or the Mob!), but the necklace was nowhere to be found.

"How could I have been so stupid?" P.J. groaned as she threw another T-shirt—a red one with *Question Authority* printed across the front—into the box on our clubhouse floor. It was Saturday, 11:45 by the clock on the wall, and the box was already filled to overflowing. "All I wanted was to solve a real crime," she said, adding Georgia Peach and Chocolate Lover to the pile. "And now . . ."

"But P.J."—I hated to hear her putting herself down. It wasn't natural. Not for P.J. Clover!—"you did what you could," I said. "You couldn't have known about Mr. Findletter's daughter. And you were right about him being up to something. It might not have been exactly what you thought," I added quickly, "but . . ."

"No," P.J. said, waving my cheery words away. "I've got to face it. I was wrong. Wrong about Mr. Findletter, wrong about Annalise. In fact, the only good thing about all this is that Tina's got her doll back and your bike is safe."

"Oh, P.J.," I cried. I'd been trying not to think about my bike, because it didn't seem fair to be happy, but now that I did . . . "Don't do it!" I exclaimed, snatching Mammoth Caves, one of my favorites, from her hand before she could dump it into the box. "It wasn't a fair bet. I don't think he even wants to win it!"

123

It was true. Even though Butch Bigelow had said exactly what I'd known he would say ("It's not that I want to do it, but I have to. A bet's a bet. . . ." etc., etc.), I could tell that after riding on the back of P.J.'s bike, after wrestling criminals and F.B.I. agents at her side, his heart wasn't in it.

"Just say he can't have them," I said.

P.J. looked shocked.

"I can't do that!" she exclaimed. "What would the world come to if people didn't stick by their word? What if ballplayers said they weren't out after three strikes, what if armies surrendered and then went on fighting, what if . . . what if the Toomey twins wrecked your bike, even though we got Tina's doll back! You wouldn't want to live in a world like that, would you? You wouldn't—"

But just then (before she could trace the end of the world to not giving Butch Bigelow her T-shirts!), there was a knock—no, a pounding—on our clubhouse door. "Open up," a voice—*two* voices—demanded.

P.J. sprang to the door. It was the Toomeys! The terrible Toomeys. Dick was standing on the steps. Tuck was eyeing my bike—my shiny blue, almost new bike—parked beside the clubhouse. He ran a grimy finger over the handlebars, leaving a greasy smudge on the chrome.

"What do you think you're doing?" P.J. demanded.

"She won't go," Dick said by way of reply.

"She's yelling and screaming," Tuck added. He gave my tire a kick.

"The camping trip's off, so . . ."

"No!" I cried, dashing down the steps and throwing

124

myself between Tuck and my bike. "She's got her doll. You can't—"

"Oh, yes we can!" Dick said. "That doll's defective. It won't eat. That's why Tina won't go on the camping trip. That's why—"

P.J. didn't give him a chance to finish. "Won't eat!" she exclaimed, a peculiar look on her face. "Stacy," she said, her voice trembling. "Maybe . . . It could be . . . It just might . . . Wait here!"

She raced into her house and returned within minutes, a black imitation-leather satchel under her arm. Before I could say a word, she dumped the satchel into my bike basket, swung her leg over the seat, and motioned for me to hop on behind. "Get Butch Bigelow," she yelled to the startled Toomey twins. "Tell him to go to your house. And hurry!"

I didn't know what was going on, and P.J. was pedaling too fast to explain. She sped down the block, around the corner, and into the Toomeys' drive, slamming on the brakes just in time to keep from crashing into the Toomeys' station wagon loaded with camping gear.

"P.J., what are you doing?" I said as she rummaged in the satchel. It was her old play doctor's kit, I suddenly realized. She dug out a headband with a fake light on it and a plastic stethoscope.

"There's no time to explain," she said as she wrapped the headband around her head and hung the stethoscope from her neck. "Just follow my lead. And if I'm right, if this works, I promise I'll never, ever make another bet with . . ."

But even as she spoke, Butch Bigelow, his face red,

his chest heaving, came running down the block. "What's going on?" he said breathlessly, skidding to a halt in the Toomeys' front yard. "Dick and Tuck told me to come over here. But it's almost noon. You've just about lost the bet. What are you . . ."

P.J. paid no attention to what he was saying. "Hold out your arm," she commanded. She pulled an armband—white with a red cross on it—from the doctor's kit, and tied it above his elbow before he could even begin to protest. "Have you got your knife?" she asked quickly.

"My knife?" Butch looked startled. He patted the pocket in his jeans where he kept his Boy Scout knife. "Yes, but . . ."

"Then come on," P.J. said, dashing up the steps and into the Toomeys' house, with Butch and me at her heels. "There's no time to lose!"

The Toomeys were in the kitchen, looking as if they'd just weathered a hurricane. Mrs. Toomey was mopping up applesauce—a whole quart of it, it seemed—from the floor. Mr. Toomey was struggling to unpack an ice chest, while holding the baby against his shoulder and wrestling a box of matches from the toddler's hand. In the midst of it all, sat Tina, her eyes red, her nose running, cradling her Baby Cuddles in her arms.

"You!" she exclaimed when she saw us, hardly seeming to notice our doctor's gear. "You're the ones who did it. You wouldn't believe me, so she got stuck in that box in that stuffy old closet and now—"

"You're right," P.J. agreed quickly. "That's why we've come to save her. Your baby, your poor baby,"

126

she crooned. She snatched Baby Cuddles from Tina's arms and before Tina could object, pressed the stethoscope against the doll's chest. She pushed a button in her back. Baby Cuddles began to move her lips in the disgusting, fishlike motion she used when she ate. At the same time, a peculiar whirring sound came from inside her stomach. P.J.'s eyes lit up. "Hear that?" she said to Tina. "That means she's sick!"

Tina, who had looked furious when P.J. grabbed her doll, melted. "That's what I've been saying," she said tearfully. "She's sick and she—"

"Needs an operation," P.J. put in quickly.

"An operation?" Tina looked bewildered. Then her eyes narrowed. "What do you mean?" she said suspiciously. "I thought you were private eyes. What do you know about operations?"

P.J. was scarcely listening. She'd glanced at the clock on the kitchen wall—11:56!—and a look of panic had come over her face. "Quick!" she said, holding her hand out to Butch. "The knife!"

"The knife?" Mrs. Toomey looked up from the applesauce.

"What knife?" said Mr. Toomey.

"This one," P.J. answered, holding the penknife that Butch, a baffled expression on his face, had handed her. "It's the only way," she said solemnly, turning to Tina. "She'll never get better unless . . ."

And suddenly I knew what she was going to do.

Suddenly I knew where the stolen necklace was!

She held the knife over Baby Cuddles' stomach. Tina screamed. Butch gasped. And it was over.

No blood of course, and there, resting in the doll's

rubbery insides—the perfect hiding place!—was the necklace. Deep blue lapis lazuli with tiny gold beads in between and a catch in the shape of a dolphin. It was lovely. And no worse for being fed to Baby Cuddles by Mr. Findletter's daughter. I could see why its owners wanted it back.

Tina stared at her baby. She looked like she was going to faint. Butch looked pale, too. He glanced at the clock. The numbers changed from 11:59 to 12:00. "You did it." He gasped. "You actually did it. And with my knife, too!"

P.J. said nothing. She simply tugged her T-shirt (her Wonder Woman T-shirt that she was going to keep!) back into place, lifted the necklace from Baby Cuddles' stomach, and handed it to me. Then, cool as any surgeon, she stretched the two flaps of rubber back into place. "Tape," she commanded, snapping her fingers.

Mrs. Toomey leaped to her feet, a look of gratitude on her face. "Brilliant," Mr. Toomey murmured as his wife dug a role of adhesive tape from a drawer and passed it to P.J. with the air of an experienced operating room nurse.

"But . . ." Tina began, still looking stunned as P.J. wound the tape around the doll's stomach. "Will she be . . . ?"

"Fresh air," P.J. declared, just as Dick and Tuck burst into the kitchen. "That's what she needs. A nice trip to the country. Camping, I think."

It wasn't easy to get out of the Toomeys' kitchen. Mr. and Mrs. Toomey kept praising us ("Brilliant," Mr. Toomey kept saying, "brilliant!"), and even Dick and Tuck managed to grunt a grudging word of thanks.

Tina was overwhelmed. "An operation," she murmured, regarding her baby's bandages with awe. "I'll have to take *extra* good care of her now."

"And feed her special food," I put in, suddenly realizing that Baby Cuddles' eating days were probably over. "Like this." I grabbed a spoon from the table and dipped it into an imaginary bowl. "See. She likes it!" I said.

Butch looked disgusted.

And he continued to look disgusted as we picked up my bike from the Toomeys' drive. "Some case," he muttered. "Some crime."

"Oh, yeah? Well you have to admit it was a *real* one!" P.J. said. "And you were pretty caught up in it, too. You weren't bad, either," she added, looking surprised at herself for saying it. "All those photos, that tape recording." She hesitated. "You don't suppose . . . ?"

Butch's cheeks turned red.

And suddenly, so did P.J.'s.

"No," she said quickly (as I let out a sigh of relief). "It would never work." She gave me a shove toward my bike, then hopped on behind as I swung my leg over the seat. "Butch Bigelow, associate associate," she said as we sped away toward our clubhouse, leaving Butch standing all by himself on the drive. "It would never fit on the door!"